"*Nothing in politics ever happens by accident. If it happens, you can bet it was planned that way.*" Quote attributed to Franklin D. Roosevelt (1882-1945) the 32nd President of the United States.

"*The world is governed by people far different from those imagined by the public.*" Quote attributed to Benjamin Disraeli (1804-1881) Prime Minister of Britain.

Fight of the American Eagles

By

Roger G Trow

0060005942

New Generation **Publishing**

Prologue

In 2050, there was a cataclysmic series of seismic events which shook the very governments and institutions of society. In the ensuing chaos dictators arose in Europe and China and under their totalitarian regimes all personal liberties were lost. But the world looked on in amazement to see the home of democracy also brought down to its knees. A man arose in the dark hour to rally America and he called for a return to the old values which had made it a great nation. Since the North American countries had all suffered and need to rebuild, he called upon the three states to unit. So, in 2052, Tyler led the way to unification. With a sense of common purpose, America, Canada and Mexico united to form the Union of the Americas. Soon afterwards the President, Benjamin Tyler declared Martial Law to quell the rioting and disorder throughout the Union and reestablished peace by a repressive dictatorship under the banner of the Freedom Party.

The people had not consented to a dictatorship and expected a benevolent and paternal leadership, but the Declaration of Emergency Powers merely brought into effect laws which had been introduced gradually through the decades by Executive Orders which handed full powers to an unelected body: The Federal Emergency Management Agency, otherwise known as FEMA.

FEMA had been handed sweeping powers to establish a police state and the military enforced the policing of the regulations. They were opposed by small groups who acted clandestinely to overthrow the government and wipe out the ruling Freedom Party. Gradually these small groups united to form a national movement-under the leadership of Duane Richards. The struggle was long and bitter, it had already continued for four decades; the government had technology and power, but the people had the will to resist. The resistance called themselves, The American Eagles.

As a result of the defeats inflicted upon him by the American Eagles, President Ben Tyler had taken his own life. He was succeeded by an even crueler man, Arturo Sanchez. Sanchez was hand in hand with the Mexican drug cartels and under his vice-presidency he had encouraged a flood tide of drugs into the society, and in anticipation of assuming the Presidency he had prepared even harsher repression for the citizens of the Union. In his greed for power, he came head on against the real power brokers, a shadowy group called The Olympians. The American Eagles fostered their mutual distrust and animosity so that the Mexicans and The Olympians met in a clash to decide who would rule the Union. Having thus drawn both parties into the same hotel in Boston, the American Eagles detonated a series of charges which killed them all. The struggle continues against their successors.

Chapter 1

David Mackintosh and his friend Nick had opted to join the resistance movement. There were few choices anyway, perhaps three: they could have joined the American Eagles in their rebellion or sat back and waited for the government of the Union of the Americas to take away what few liberties remained after forty years of martial law; or even to sell-out and become collaborators. The third option was not even to be considered by any honest man and the second seemed highly improbable to have a good outcome. You might say that the degree of freedom for their choice, in all practicality, was reduced to one course.

Every week, it seemed, the government of Ian Sharpe issued new decrees aimed at tightening central control over the population. The civilian population of the Americas were corralled into their cities and not allowed any of the personal freedoms that their fathers had taken so much for granted. Martial Law gave the military absolute power of arrest and the Courts were subjugated to the authority of the Regional Military Commanders. The rule of law was nominally subject to the Emergency Powers Bill, but in practice it was arbitrary and the Court's judgments were meaningless

Sharp had come to power following the deaths of his predecessors, Presidents Ben Tyler and Arturo Sanchez: Tyler had committed suicide, while Sanchez had been assassinated along with the entire Board of the Olympians. Sharp, however, was a more prudent man. He had bided his time and allowed Tyler and Sanchez to build the system that established the Freedom Party in complete control over the Americas.

They had made their mistakes and it had cost them their lives.

Tyler had allowed the American Eagles to take a strategic advantage in a guerilla war and, in so doing; he earned the displeasure of his paymasters, The Olympians.

His successor, Arturo Sanchez had also crossed The Olympians by trespassing upon their business interests, mainly the drug trade, but also he had disrespected them and tried to usurp their strategy for the New World Order. Ian Sharp had no doubt that the American Eagles had been responsible for the assassinations, since it suited their aims to remove both parties. He deduced that there was no one else, except possibly himself, to benefit from Sanchez' removal from power, and he took full advantage of the opportunity. Unlike his predecessors, Sharpe believed in the New World Order and he was an ardent Luciferian. In the New World everything would be neat and tidy. He would see to it that all of that messy political legacy would be removed. Democracy was a failed system of government and only one step removed from anarchy in its purest form. Freedom meant the choice to obey or disobey, nothing else made any sense to Sharpe's cold analytical mind. Slowly, but inexorably, the loopholes that allowed any personal freedoms were being closed; and by the consent of The Olympians, Ian Sharp governed and faithfully implemented their policies.

David Mackintosh had had a successful career in the media as a news anchor at The All-American News Station, but when Supreme Court Justice Duane Richards approached him to join the struggle, he had accepted the offer gladly, and now, with the technical assistance of his friend Nick, he had the opportunity to do some real investigative journalism. Duane had procured documents for them that permitted free movement across provincial and district borders; they were impossible to replicate and as rare as hen's teeth, but they had never failed to pass at the Inter-Provincial security checkpoints.

Today they were travelling east from Rapid City, South Dakota towards Mitchell by way of the Interstate 90. In passing through Rapid City, they had seen for themselves the results of the New World Order upon the citizens. People moved along the streets aimlessly, work was rarely available and the only thing that was cheap and easy to obtain were the Mexican's street drugs. People took the drugs so that they could forget the hopelessness of life; to forget the screams in the night as their neighbors were dragged from their beds and taken away to detainee camps. They were told that these folk had been foreign sleeper agents, but who could believe it of lifetime friends, and to whom could one protest?

Occasionally a party of men and women could be seen working on the roads, they were carrying out maintenance work, but when they looked up their eyes showed no human awareness, they worked like autonomic machines: they were the Robotoids. This was the fate of those who resisted the New World Order and ultimately it would be the fate of the world labor force: to be stripped of their humanity by chemical injections and mind control; mindless beasts fit only to serve the needs of the elite class.

Normally, David and Nick avoided the main routes and looked for good secondary roads, but this route did at least have the advantage of two national parks where they might sleep over in their camper, instead of staying at a popular hotel or motel. Nick fancied the Badlands National Park but David convinced him to drive a little further to the Buffalo Gap National Grasslands.

There was no particular reason to choose the turnoff onto County Road Ch 13, but it seemed as good as any other in the rolling wilderness area. Their all-terrain tyres and turbo-drive to all wheels made the Ventura the ideal vehicle for their purposes. So when they saw the sign pointing off the county road to a lake, it seemed that it would be the logical place to pitch camp. The Ventura was a low profile truck with a collapsible habitat section and an extending rear end that creates a spacious living room. They were fully independent, with a generator -powered furnace for cold weather and an air-conditioner for the hot seasons. Nick had also taken care to replace all of the truck's chrome fittings on the external bodywork with matt -painted plastic trims, and the panels were constructed of a special material that resisted radar detection; so other than the windshield, they wouldn't attract the attention of routine surveillance drones. The road undulated and there was very little tree cover, only the occasional tall thorn bush grew along the road. As they gradually approached the summit of one of the hills, David suddenly shouted, "Stop! Back up a bit!"

Nick immediately slammed on the brakes and the Ventura slid to a halt on the gravelly surface of the road. "What? What is it, Bud?" He asked.

"I saw something ahead. Drive the vehicle behind that tall bush, over there." David indicated a large thorny bush next to the road. "Bring the telescope and the video attachment, Nick, I saw something just down in the valley south of the road. Better keep your head down!"

They approached the crest of the bank stealthily, and they lay flat on their fronts as they surveyed the valley below. Down the slopes, and well-nigh in sight of the Interstate, was a large field. It had been grazing land for a herd of beef cattle; but no more, for they were all dead. A hundred or more cows lay dead in the grassland, some of the animals were on their sides and others lay with their legs grotesquely pointing into the air. Clearly they had died in agony. Nick slowly panned across the field; his lens zoomed in on some of the carcasses. In the digital display screen there was evidence that, prior to death, the cows had frothed at the mouth. At the far side of the field, near the highway, some men were loading carcasses into trucks with frontloading mechanical shovels. They were all dressed in military uniforms, but over them they wore special bio-hazard suits. One of the soldiers forgot himself and thinking to have quick cigarette, he began fiddling with his helmet, but a shout from the sergeant made him close up his visor quickly.

As Nick panned across the upper field, he noticed some white cylindrical containers about the size of domestic water heaters. The vessels had domed tops but their lids were opened and in one case it could be seen that the tank was completely empty. Nick indicated that they had to leave immediately, so they wriggled back until they were below the brow of the hill and then they ran back to the camper.

"Let's get the hell out of here, David! I'll explain as we go!" Nick hurriedly turned the truck and keeping the engine on low revs, they carefully returned down the gravel road until they reached the junction with the County Road. Nick pulled over and turning to David he said, "Buddy, we have just had a very lucky escape!"

"Nick, what was it that killed the cattle, was it something from those white tanks?"

"Yes, it was. And it was lucky for us that the wind was blowing down the hill, or we'd be dead now! One of those soldiers in the work detail almost got himself killed, and if it hadn't been for his sergeant he's be as dead now as those poor cows. You see, those tanks are something that I'd heard of when I was in the Signals Corps. It was whispered about, you know? They are known as Cluster Bomb Units or CBU's for short. Each cluster bomb may contain a powerful nerve gas or high explosive. They were originally developed at the turn of the century for use against massed militants or rioting civilians. They are dropped from drones by parachute into a zone where militants are concentrated. They are totally illegal, of course; we signed international treaties long ago that forbade their use, but try telling Ian Sharp or the Joint Chiefs of Staff that! These are their weapons of last resort, if the American Eagles ever mounted a mass attack. I am sure that Duane's military advisors are well aware of them, so that is why we are using guerilla tactics only; it takes longer, but we are wearing down the dictatorship slowly but surely!"

"Hmm, then this may not have been an accidental discharge, such as a CBU falling from a military transport! No, Nick, there were several tanks in the field, and they were all set in a line; one on its own might be an accident. How many did you count?"

Nick replied grimly, "I made it four, and they *were* lying in a straight line. No, David, this was a field test. Either they were checking on the potency of an old

12

batch or they were trying out a new formula. Callous bastards! I wonder if they even bothered to get the rancher's permission first, probably not."

"Then, I vote we drive on and clear the area, before they make a security sweep and stop us. Our surveillance equipment might take some explaining, especially in the present circumstances!"

Nick drove carefully back to the highway to rejoin the eastward bound traffic, soon they had merged into the flow. When they reached a point south of the test site, a military diversion had been set up to take Interstate traffic a long way south of the highway, but the lights of the military vehicles could be seen afar off, working on in the gathering dusk. "It was good that we didn't hang around, Nick, our lights would have been a dead giveaway."

"Yes, as they say, 'He who turns and runs away shall live to fight another day!'"

Ten minutes later on and the lights of Kadoka Municipal Airport came into view. Now it was commonly used as a local military staging area and there were constant aerial movements throughout the day, according to their intelligence briefing notes. Perhaps it was connected with the action that they had witnessed down the road. Several hovers took off together and passed overhead silently. One of them peeled off from the formation and flew along the highway, David knew that the RFID's on all vehicles were being scanned automatically, but he wasn't concerned because they personally had impeccable RFID's and the licence plates of the Ventura matched an identical vehicle with a South Dakota registration. The hover paused above a truck three places behind them and the drone issued the standard instruction for the truck to pull over. A human highway patrol would soon arrive to investigate the anomaly. That was how the fascists operated. Sure enough, within five minutes, a patrol car of the South Dakota Brigade roared past, heading for the luckless motorist.

One rarely saw anyone on foot along the highways anymore, only the occasional work gangs of citizens pressed into 'community service' or Robotoids who had no freedom of choice anyway. The Badlands were an inhospitable area for a breakdown, and Nick always did a full check of the tires and the engine's mechanics before they set off in the morning.

"What do you think, Nick, it's kinda active hereabouts, and so shall we press on? There are several more airports situated along this route, and security may be higher than usual at all of them. We might find somewhere nearby Chamberlain where we can pull over. There's a River Missouri bridge crossing there and there is sure to be a tourist park campsite nearby."

"Yes, I agree. It would be best to avoid parking along the main road. It's not permitted on the Interstate, but I wouldn't want to chance it on any of the highways either. In a tourist campsite, we will be lost among the other campers." Nick punched Chamberlain Township into his comm. link. "The map says that there's a recreation area, just north of the Interstate 90 Business Route crossing of the Missouri River, it's called 'American Creek'. It's pretty old and it might be a bit run-down but that should suit us just fine: not too many other campers would choose an old park and the cops won't bother us in an off the main track site either. Mitchell is not too far from Chamberlain Township, but I'd rather avoid the towns, wouldn't you, especially after what we saw at Rapid City?"

David nodded, "Then we will make Sioux Falls tomorrow? That's an easy drive. I'll call up the area commander and let him know that we are right on schedule. The word is that they have collected some very interesting intelligence about the FEMA camp at Sioux Falls. When we add the videos that we have collected to that, we have another great propaganda piece to splash across the networks. "

Nick grinned. "I'll just bet that Sharp is tearing his hair out, wondering just how we manage to bypass all of his firewalls to broadcast to the nation. Even to a population as cowed down as the Union of the Americas, the truth must eventually break through."

"Yes, it will. But don't forget that our broadcasts are also watched by the armed forces and their commanders. I've heard that defections are increasing and in some cities they can hardly muster a brigade anymore and they have been forced to supplement the foot patrols with surveillance drones flying at low altitude!"

The American Creek Recreational Park looked as if it was closed, and it had actually seen better days. It consisted of a few barbecue sites with hookups for trailer homes. Probably a hundred trailers had once used the park. Nick parked the Ventura in the parking lot, just in front of the office. David knocked at the superintendent's door and finally his repeated knocking brought a response. From within, there was the sound of shuffling feet and a chink in the curtain told him that someone was checking him out. Then there was the sound of a key turning in the lock and a double-barrel shotgun poked out; it was pointed directly at David's chest. "We're closed, can't you see?" A sharp querulous voice said, "What do you want, coming by here at this time? We are closed!" The woman repeated.

"Ma'am, there's no need to be alarmed. We're respectable folk. It's just me and my buddy. We're passing through, you know. We'll be off in the morning; we only need a place to park the camper, that's all. We can't camp on the roadside or the patrols will give us a hard time. We won't be any trouble. There's no need to be pointing a gun at me."

"Fifty bucks! And don't make any noise, I'm a light sleeper."

"Did you say, fifty bucks?" David asked with some surprise.

"Yes, fifty bucks. Take it or leave it!"

With a sigh, David reached for his wallet and she opened the door a mite wider. She was a woman in her thirties, hair pulled back in a tight bun and she wore a long, somewhat shabby dress that would have fitted well in a period drama about the old Wild West. She reached for the money and snatched it quickly from David's hand.

"Can't be too careful these days," she said, by way of apology for her rude behaviour, "there have been some robberies at night around here. They say that it's illegals on the run; I expect that they are just travelers on tough times, looking for food, poor devils. No one got hurt though; they broke into a couple of food stores across in the township and someone stole a few eggs from a farm. I can't blame them, no, not if they're hungry. But a body's got to be careful, especially a woman who's alone."

"Well, we will keep a look out for you, ma'am. My buddy is quite useful if it comes to a rough and tumble, and I can handle myself well. Now, you don't worry!

Just lock your door now, and we will park over there under the trees. We'll be near enough if you need us, but not so near as to disturb you. I'll bid you goodnight then, ma'am."

David walked back to the Ventura and Nick drove it across to the trees where they picked out a position that gave them a view of the office buildings as well as the entrance driveway. "Nick, I think that trouble just seems to follow us. She is one nervous lady! There have been some robberies around here and that's why she pointed the shotgun at me. It must a museum piece, but I've no doubt that it could make a serious hole in someone at that range!"

Ten minutes later, and they had raised the camper's roof height and erected the dining extension unit. Soon Nick had coffee brewing, and David made up some sandwiches from their tinned rations, so they used up the last of the bread. "Nick, tomorrow, we'll buy fresh bread in Chamberlain. Hopefully, they won't require seeing our ration cards in such a small place as this. I only have our New Washington ones with me, I clean forgot about the small purchases like bread. Worse comes to worse, we'll have to eat in restaurants or hotels, or we'll have to cook rice on the gas stove. That will be alright for you though, it'll be just like you days in the forces when you ate beans out of Dixie tins and ground your own coffee from acorns. " Nick punched him playfully.

"No problem, Buddy, there's little chance of us starving; we've hauled a huge weight of canned food across three states too. The more we eat, the lighter the camper gets!" They both laughed.

In the wee hours, David was awakened by the sound of feet outside the camper. He quietly woke up Nick and, grabbing their laser pistols, they emerged from the camper. There was a scurrying in the darkness, but David's flashlight caught the intruders in its beam. "Stay where you are," he ordered, "we are armed and we will shoot! Come here with your hands raised."

Three figures approached the camper. It was a man, a woman and a little child. They were dressed in ragged clothes and even by the light of the torch, it could be seen that they were very grubby and their hair looked unkempt. "What are you doing here?" Nick demanded

"Sir, please don't shoot us! We just came looking for food; we haven't eaten for three days." The voice was that of a woman, but it was spoken in an odd monotone. Nick swept his light up and down them, they seemed to be unarmed and without baggage, except for the little boy who carried a small teddy bear in his arms.

"Then you had better come inside, before you wake up the manageress and she calls the cops. Come in here. Take a seat and tell us what happened to you, that you should be wandering the back roads of Chamberlain scavenging for food."

The woman was in her twenties, her dark brown hair was in a proper tangle and her face was streaked with grime. The coat that she wore was an old overcoat, just like they used to wear before the new materials came onto the market. The man and the boy were like peas in a pod, clearly this was a family unit. Their clothes too were torn and faded. Nick went into the pantry to get them something to eat because they looked as if they were starving. David poured three glasses of milk and they gulped them down as if they were parched.

"Come sit down here and eat first," David said to them kindly," you look all done in." Without replying, they accepted the opportunity to rest and then Nick returned with some cans of beef sausage and some beans. He poured the food onto some plates and they wolfed it down silently, using their hands and fingers. Finally, they finished everything. David looked closely at them. They were pasty-white skinned, which you wouldn't expect of people living out on the road, but they were otherwise fairly normal in their appearance, yet there was something about them that just made David uncomfortable. Perhaps it was the way that they carried themselves, and their eyes were odd too, they seemed somehow fixed and unfocused. A thought suddenly occurred to him. He called to Nick, "Hey Buddy, make up some more drinks would you? You know that *special* milk drink that you know I like so much?" Nick poked his head around the doorway, with a quizzical look on his face. David rarely drank whole milk, except in a cappuccino coffee. Then Nick got the message and nodded, before returning to the kitchen range. Soon the sound of the blender could be heard.

"So what are your names?" David asked the man. The man replied with a blank look; this was getting weird. He repeated the question, but all three of them just sat looking at him without a word or a change of expression. "I order you to answer the question, what are your names?" Nick overheard the order and he stood in the doorway looking at David, with surprise on his face. The man suddenly seemed to come awake and he addressed David in the same flat tone that the woman had used earlier.

"Sir, I am Bob Leasing, this is my wife Amy and my son Jonathan. We have been on the road for two weeks, mostly walking but hitching a ride when we could. We are so grateful for your help; I think we were about done in until we met you. We are honest folk, sirs, but still it's only fair to tell you that we are fugitives, through no fault of our own though. I am telling you this because we don't want you to get into trouble for harboring us. We would like to stay a while and then we will be on our way." There was scarcely a pause between the sentences and he spoke as if from memory.

David considered his answer for a moment and then he asked, "When did you last sleep in a bed?"

Bob Leasing replied again in that monotone, "Sir, that would be about ten days ago. A farmer put us up for the night, we were planning to sleep in his barn, but the dogs caught our scent and he found us. I guess he didn't think it right for Jonathan to sleep rough. We didn't stay long there, just two days, and then we moved on. That's mostly how it has been. We keep moving; often we travel at night when the hovers aren't patrolling."

It was a strange manner of speech. There was nothing particularly improper, except it was as if he had learned the dialogue off pat. David's sense of unease was growing. He decided to probe the man a little more. "What is your business, Bob?"

"I used to work in the radio station, I was the sound engineer for WQVS in Rapid City. We are heading for Sioux City because we heard that there is work there."

"Oh, then you know Bob Hartles, the Station Manager and Philip Sims the General Manager at WQVS?"

"Yes, sir, I knew them well before I lost my job and had to leave."

Nick entered the room, bearing a tray with three large glasses of milkshake on it. "Well, look here," Nick exclaimed, "if you want to stay tonight, that's alright by us. We can talk in the morning and see what needs to be done. But you won't sleep in a barn or a ditch tonight! Oh, no! Look, we have camping rolls and you can sleep here on the floor. But don't go outside in the morning light, the manager might see you and file a report. Is that OK?" They nodded in that same deadpan way. "Here are some drinks. Drink them now!" He ordered. They immediately obeyed his bidding and downed the milk drinks in one. Nick added, "I'll sort some clean clothes out for you all later, but meanwhile we have a shower unit inside and you can wash some of that grime off your bodies. I'll put some soap in there for you too. You take off those dirty clothes."

They stood up and where they were, they began to disrobe, including the woman. First, their topcoats and then the shirts and pants, even their underwear. Then they stood motionless in the middle of the floor, butt naked, but apparently unaware of it. The woman turned to Nick as he had been the one who had ordered them to undress. "Do you wish to have sex with me now or after the shower?"

Nick was taken aback and he replied hurriedly, "No, not at all, not now or later! Go and take your showers, and clean your bodies well, so there will be no smell." Immediately, they turned as one and filed into the shower unit and soon the sound of running water could be heard. Nick peeped inside and they were simply standing under the shower without moving. "Wash your bodies with the soap!" He ordered. He returned to the living area where David was busy flicking over some files that he had stored on his comm. link. "David, what the hell's going on?"

David looked up from his scanning and turning to Nick, he said just one word, "Robotoids!"

"Robotoids? You mean all three of them are robotoids? I can see that something is not right about them. But I thought that the government had confined all Robotoids to the factories as a labour force for the Olympians? So what are Robotoids doing walking out here in the countryside about Chamberlain? And how come that Bob leasing knew those folks at the radio station, I thought that Robotoids were brainless."

"That, my dear friend is a very, very good question. And it is one that we shall find the answer to shortly. As for the two men that I mentioned, they don't exist, I made the names up. My guess is that they are giving programmed responses to certain types of questions. But they are certainly not brainless as you put it. It seems that certain moral switches are switched off and they are programmed to obey orders that override their power to choose. Did you put a strong dose of barbiturates in their drinks? So, when they are asleep, we will examine them carefully, even their cavities, I'm afraid! And let's not forget little teddy bear and the pendants that they carry about their necks. You do a sweep of all three of them and let's do the bear first. I have a strong suspicion that Teddy is no ordinary bear!" he smiled grimly.

"David, is all of this absolutely necessary? I'd hate to do this and find out that you were wrong. It's sort of a violation, you know, like rape!"

"Nick, you also discerned that there was something odd about them. And you also picked up that they only respond when addressed by orders from a superior. In fact when they come to, I may dig more into these fake personas and we shall reconfirm our suspicions. One more thing, Buddy, don't forget that our enemy is wily and unscrupulous, they wouldn't hesitate to inject mind control chemicals into children or adults for that matter. In fact, I'll tell you; my hunch is that they have been programmed to entrap unwary travellers or homeowners by begging for help, which is against the emergency laws!"

Nick returned to the camper shower unit. The water had been switched off and the Leasing family stood outside it awaiting their next order. The woman was quite beautiful, now that she was clean, her long brown hair hung in attractive curls down to her shoulders but her eyes were expressionless as she returned his gaze. It saddened Nick to think that some monster had transformed her into an automaton fit only to unthinkingly execute commands, however demeaning.

"Here," he said brusquely, "now put on these clean clothes and then come into the other room. Do not make any noise unless we speak to you." They quickly dressed and then followed Nick back into the habitat area. David had arranged the bedrolls on the floor. The family was very tired and could hardly stay awake. "You lie down and go to sleep now. Lie on your backs." They complied with his order immediately. In a few minutes they were all deeply asleep.

"Nick, let's start with the bug sweeper shall we?" Nick went to fetch it from the storage cabinet in the camper. David remained to keep a watchful eye on their guests, but they never moved a muscle, but slept with a deep rhythmic pattern, their eyes remained open and unblinking. It was eerie. Each of the pendants showed an electrical response to the sweeper, so Nick carefully removed them and placed each pendant in some insulated, anti-static envelopes that he used when carrying memory chips or materials sensitive to magnetic fields. Then he swept the Teddy bear. It was alive! Slicing it open carefully, Nick found that it was full of circuitry, he recognized a tracking device, and it even had a receiver. Nick guessed that the bear was a link to the controller in a security force office nearby, but certainly someplace in the State of South Dakota if it had a satellite uplink. There was no mechanism to record conversations, but Nick guessed that Bob Leasing, if that was his name, would send messages when he completed an assignment. He placed the bear carefully in a sack; it would not be good thing if it instantly went off the air. The electronic body scans revealed nothing, and since the woman had offered sex, they assumed that nothing would be gained by investigating her cavities; which was a relief to both of them.

"And now, Nick, we call it in. I'll go outside and call up our contact in the city, and get his instructions. Can you stay here and keep a watch on the three of them? Call me if they stir!"

"Yes, I'll do that. They don't look likely to wake anytime soon, David, may I overdid the barbiturates? It would be real embarrassing if they didn't wake up again. We'd have to drop them in the Missouri River." Nick sniggered at his own humor.

'Buddy, don't even joke about it!" he admonished Nick.

David took his comm. link outside the camper and placed an urgent encrypted call to the American Eagles' area commander in Sioux Falls. It was well past midnight, but his call was answered promptly.

Chapter 2

"Hi, sorry to call you at such a late hour, but we have an emergency. We are in the American Creek Recreational Park, at Chamberlain. We had some late night visitors, a man, a woman and a small boy child. They are Robotoids, but don't worry, they are all under sedation; however, we don't know what to do with them. Can you assist us?"

"I'm sorry; did you say that you have actually *captured* three Robotoids? That's impossible. No one has ever captured one alive. They carry a self-destruct device on their bodies, usually on a chain about the neck. In fact, if it is known that they are in imminent danger of being captured, the security command controller will initiate the self-destruct sequences and the Robotoids' heads will be blown off. Did you secure the explosive devices and what about the portable controller's device? The controller's device might be hidden in an article that they are carrying with them."

"The three explosive devices are in separate insulated bags. We found the portable controller's device inside a toy bear that the small boy was carrying. We have kept it in a sack, as we didn't want to tip off the security force that their operatives had been compromised."

"Well, that all sounds fine. Now look, the manageress of the recreational park is one of ours. She will cover you until we get there. I will call her to inform what has happened. Don't leave the park and don't let the Robotoids escape. This is an amazing coup! We will leave here within the hour. I have passes that permit me to travel after the curfew time, so we shall make good time. I shall have medics with me, and they will take care of the family. See you around eight o'clock or earlier if possible. Try to get some sleep, tomorrow is going to be a long day, or so I'm guessing."

David returned to the camper, where he found everything was still normal, Nick was sitting on a chair with his feet up on another chair, but he was wide awake. As David entered, he sprang to his feet. "So, what's the news, David?"

David sat in the chair facing Nick and replied quietly, "Well, I made contact, even though it was so late, but the area commander was very helpful. It seems that these Robotoids are programmed to self-destruct if they get cornered, so what we did was unprecedented and absolutely the safest course. Those pendants that you recovered from around their necks are explosive devices and, if they were to be detonated, they would take the wearer's head off! They can be triggered manually or remotely by the portable controller's device that was stashed inside the boy's bear, which is linked to the local security command. In fact, this is the very first time that anyone has managed to isolate the explosive devices or the portable link, so the commander was ecstatic. They are on their way here now, and they expect to arrive at the latest by eight o'clock, depending upon the checkpoints en-route, I suppose."

Nick resumed his seat and dropped his voice to a loud whisper, "We'll take turns in keeping watch then. Three hours apiece ought to be OK, there's no telling what the Leasing family might do if they woke up and found their pendants and the bear missing. From the way that she offered sex in such a matter of fact way, I'm sure that all moral codes are suppressed by the programming, and they might do anything to us if they caught us both sleeping!"

"I think that we can go one better than just standing guard over them. Let's tie their legs together with some of your long cable grips. That way, they can't walk away, and if they wake and ask us why we tied them up, we will tell them that we were following orders from the security control officer. They don't know anything about us, and they are conditioned to obey orders from a superior."

Nick quickly tied their legs and tethered the chain to the frame of the habitat. "There, that ought to alert us if they try to get free!" he said with some satisfaction. David made himself comfortable on a mat next to Nick and Nick lowered the lights.

The vigil went without incident, and the trio of Robotoids slept on; they had been genuinely exhausted, David reflected. "Poor devils! I wonder how long they have wandered the countryside? Were they looking for strangers whom they would eventually betray for showing them small kindnesses? What kind of inhumane people would think up such a ploy, let alone inflict such a mutilation upon a fellow human being?" Nick was awake and had a cup of coffee ready for David. It was good medicine to fight off the early morning chill in the Dakotas.

At seven thirty, they heard the sound of vehicles driving along the gravel driveway. David slipped his laser pistol behind his back, and he peeped out to see who had arrived. The newcomers were the local American Eagles, they drove an ambulance and a large gray all -terrain vehicle.

The manageress of the Recreational Park came out to meet them, and she had a quick conversation with a bald headed guy who was dressed in a white medical gown. She pointed across the park to the Ventura and then went back inside. David walked outside, leaving Nick to stand watch over the Leasing family who were still sleeping. "Hi, you must be David Mackintosh, I guess? I'm Dr. John Phillips, we spoke last night. How are the prisoners?"

"Glad to meet you, Doctor." David replied, "They are secure. My partner, Nick, hit them with a powerful dose of barbiturate in a flavoured milk drink. They went to sleep after midnight, which is when I called you. They are still asleep; I hope that we didn't overdo the drug. We also tied them together, so in case they awoke, they wouldn't be able to run away or attack us. Come inside and see for yourself. I'll give you a tip for dealing with them, if they wake up, just speak to them as if you were their superior and they will obey your commands. They are probably used to receiving orders from people dressed in white coats too."

"Hmm, that's good to know. You've done a great job guys! I'll have my team handle them from here on. We will take them back to Sioux Falls as if they were emergency cases. I'll zap them again to make sure that they appear to be comatose. Chances are that they are very drug tolerant, as the regime must be dosing them regularly to maintain the chemical programming."

He whistled to his medics and waved them across to the habitat space of the camper. Minutes later, they emerged with the three Robotoids strapped onto gurneys, and they quickly transferred the Leasing family to the ambulance. "By the way, David, I'd advise that you leave here immediately. We can't be sure whether the security controller monitors the Robotoids' position on a regular basis. Once we leave, you ought to leave soon after; you can follow us at a discreet distance. If the regime comes sniffing around here, the manageress has been briefed what to say. She will tell them that there were some intruders who broke into her store and stole some food during the night." As he spoke, there was the sound of a glass window being broken in one of the outbuildings.

David replied, "We will leave here in five to ten minutes. We will catch you up but remain at least a mile behind you, in case there are any hover drones patrolling the Interstate."

"Oh, you can be sure of that. There is constant surveillance of the highway, as it is a major transit route through the Mid-West area. There seems to be a particular alert on at the moment, but we didn't see anything as we were coming here. I will give you all the background about the regime's activities when we are safely in Sioux Falls, but let's get away from here quickly. Don't stop anywhere and don't pick up any hitch-hikers, and you should be alright. You can't trust anyone these days, as you have just found out. When we get to Sioux Falls, we will close formation, and you can follow me to our base. Take it easy, guys!"

As David had predicted, it only took five minutes for him and Nick to disassemble the habitat and get ready to depart. As they rolled out of the parking area, the curtain in the office window twitched, but the manageress didn't show herself. "I hope that we didn't bring trouble down upon her head." David said softly.

The countryside east of the township boundary was open rolling grasslands, rather like savannah. You could see for miles in any direction, but the downside of the topography was that, if a security patrol came looking for you, there would be nowhere to hide. Nick gunned the Ventura's powerful engine, and they were soon speeding along at the maximum permitted speed.

In a short while, however, they spotted the medical convoy ahead, and after they had closed the gap to about a mile, Nick eased back and maintained the speed to match that of the convoy's.

As they passed south of Kimball Municipal Airport, a couple of hovers circled around to check on the early travelers, but once again, the plates and RFID on the Ventura satisfied the security check, and they soon lost interest, and resumed their patrol westward along the highway. North and south of the Interstate, the grasslands gave way to small to medium sized homesteads, and from Mitchell eastwards, there was little interstate traffic; but farm vehicles could be seen moving along Old Highway 15 and other roads that ran parallel to the Interstate Highway. "I wonder what it's like living under the shadow of all this surveillance?" David said to Nick.

"Yeh, it kinda jars against living here in these wide open spaces!" he replied.

I 90 passed through the southern suburbs of Mitchell, but the town was strangely quiet; it was as quiet as a ghost town. There ought to be some signs of life on the streets. David had a sense of foreboding. It was almost as if the township had been evacuated. David looked up the town in his gazetteer of the Mid-West, the data was about ten years old, but the population was stated to be 20,000. So where was everybody? David had never heard any whispers about an evacuation of the area, not even during his days as a news anchor for All-American News in New York. How could such a thing have happened? He shared his thoughts with Nick.

"I guess we know now what those gas cluster bombs were used for apart from killing off a herd of beef!"

Nick replied. "No, do you really think that the regime is capable of such an act. Why that is genocide. How low they have sunk! That they could have eradicated an entire town, at a stroke! And what is also worrying, David, how was it done behind a veil of secrecy?"

"These are questions that Dr. John Phillips may know the answers to. Keep driving, Nick; and I'll keep the camera rolling. Let's get some record of this for the nation to see!" David zoomed in on the town, and his lens swept the deserted streets and public areas that were visible from the Interstate. "I suppose that the environment is still toxic from the gas. Do you happen to know how long it is dangerous, Nick?"

"Well, there are many environmental factors to consider. Some gases leave little residue behind, and some are neutralized by rainwater or solar radiation. I'm guessing that an urban area would be hazardous for thirty days at least. We don't know when this occurred, but look, there are no birds in the skies, and I'll bet that the James River ahead is just full of dead fish. No, we won't be stopping, David, much as I'd like to, but I value my health more than your story, Bud!"

"No, it's alright, you just keep driving. I guess that was why Dr. John told us not to stop along the way." They slowed down as they crossed the James River Bridge, David zoomed his camera lens down along the banks of the river where there was a silvery thread along the water's edge. "Those are dead fish, Nick. I can zoom right in on them from this elevation. Why, the runoff from the town of Mitchell must have polluted the whole of this stretch of the river. That chemical must be so toxic. What madness! Come, let's not linger. I think I understand now just why there is so much aerial activity in this area at the moment."

He put the camera down and Nick resumed their cruising speed.

It was just in time, as at that moment a hover drone overflew them. From the James River eastwards, the country gave way to rolling grassland again, and the Interstate highway was mostly long, monotonous straights with a few bends to relieve the tedium. David took a spell at driving, while Nick took an opportunity to catch up on some sleep. Soon they reached the outskirts of the city of Sioux Falls. Roadside billboard signs directed the tourists of another era toward the Big Sioux River and Sioux Falls, from which the city is named. In former days, the amazing gorge down which the Sioux River plunges had drawn tourists from far and wide, but nowadays few people troubled themselves with the hassle of obtaining an internal visa that would permit them to travel interstate. The result was that the fine city was dying from the absence of the tourist revenue. The broad streets in the suburbs of Sioux Falls were almost deserted of traffic, and the main road had numerous potholes. They guessed that the lack of local traffic was due to the fact that in these depressed times few could afford the price of gas when their income had dried up. The only industries still functioning were connected with the manufacture of furniture and paneling for house construction, but it was definitely a depressed economy without the tourist dollars coming in. Nick and David had seen the same depressing picture throughout their travels: east or west, north and south in the former USA and in Mexico and Canada too, everyone was hurting. But when would they arise and overthrow the tyrants? No, until the American Eagles showed them the way, the population would continue to suffer the oppression passively.

They caught up with Dr. John and the ambulance just after the outskirts of the city. They were parked beneath a sign which pointed to the Central Hospital. Could this be their destination? David began to sweat. What if this had all been an elaborate trap? Well, there was nothing for it now but to play along and see what the outcome would be!

The convoy entered the Central Hospital, and the ambulance followed the road that led to the emergency and trauma centre entrance. Dr. John waved to David and indicated that they should follow his vehicle. He led them around to a quiet area at the rear of the hospital, there was an underground car park, and they entered it. Dr. John indicated that they could park in the area designated as the 'Doctors' Reserved Parking Area'.

"Welcome to my humble abode", he said with a slight bow. "Let's talk when we are inside." He led the way through three sets of doors with numeric key pad locks and CCTV camera coverage. The corridor continued on into the hospital medical wards and administration offices, but Dr. John paused at the elevator. When the elevator arrived, he inserted a key into the keypad and then pressed '02'. The elevator descended two floors below the basement level. "To all intents and appearances this elevator only rises from the basement, but if you insert the key, it takes you down to the heart of our operation." He explained. "What could be better than having our HQ right under the nose of the Regime?" He added with a chuckle. "Come into my office, please."

They followed him through into a large operations room. Some men and women were working at computer consoles, and others were monitoring military communications. "We were lucky enough to capture a drone the other day. It had an engine malfunction and dropped right in front of one of our patrols. We snatched it away before the security forces could send a salvage team. Now we have learned the frequency of their broadcasts to the drones, we can jam the terrestrial signals. But we plan to hijack their satellite too, and then it will get real interesting. Probably, we will capture a lot more using that information, and not only here in South Dakota, but over the whole of the Union. Do you realize what this means? We estimate that there are 50,000 drones flying around the Americas. Many of these can carry a payload of explosives or surveillance equipment. We will bomb the military with their own hardware, we may even gas them with their own cluster bombs, if we can get some, and we can certainly discover more of their dirty little secrets using these drones!

And now for the icing on the cake: you have just caught three of the Robotoids and the portable control unit! Just think what we may be able to do with them, once we have examined them. We won't use them as weapons, oh no! But maybe we can reverse the damage done to their brains by the chemical therapy. I'd love it if we could capture even one of the monsters who mutilated them. I can tell you, I'd have no compunction whatsoever in squeezing every last drop of information from their brains! The portable controller units also operate via an uplink to a satellite; that much we know already. I'm a doctor of medicine, so this is a bit out of my field, but our technical experts say that we might be able to use the signal from your portable controller unit to send a virus to the satellite. If we can disable the satellite or hijack it and change the access codes, who knows what chaos it will create for the military? They have had it too easy for too long! Now we are going to put them on the receiving end of their own weaponry."

He spoke with such passion, it was clear that the abuses of the military and their bosses, the Olympians, just sickened him. David decided that now was as good a time as any to raise the issue of what they had seen in Mitchell.

"Doctor John, on our way here we couldn't help noticing the strange absence of all signs of life in Mitchell township. And earlier we had witnessed the military cleaning up a chemical test site, west of Mitchell. We saw Cluster Bomb Units and a whole herd of dead cattle. As we drove past Mitchell this morning, we noticed that there was not as much as a bird to be seen from the Interstate. So without stopping, we filmed the deserted suburbs of Mitchell; and also all along the James River banks where we saw thousands of dead fish. Have they used gas on the town, and if so, why?"

Suddenly, Dr. John looked terribly sad, and he had to sit down before he could speak, they each sat beside him. "I can see why you are a successful journalist, David. You see what others might miss. What happened in Mitchell is a closely guarded secret and amounts to an act of genocide. What we know is fragmentary; we have had to piece together bits of information from various sources, from eavesdropping on security force communications or from military men coming into the hospital for treatment- under anesthetic people often talk unknowingly about things that trouble them. Anyway this is all we know; the population of Mitchell was selected as a test subject for a new implant, a microchip that would compel the citizen to register his presence wherever he went; the chip would contain all of his vital information, including his financial holdings. It would function like a RFID badge does, but it would do much, much more than that. The town was cordoned off while the citizens were being canvassed for their participation in the project. The citizens rejected the notion of being micro-chipped like animals. Neither did they trust the military's promise that by accepting the chip, life would be much simpler because they wouldn't need to carry cash or credit cards which can be lost or stolen. So to a man, the town refused to accept the chip. From what we can discover, this 100% refusal so enraged the Regime that they ordered the military to drop a type of cluster bomb that contains a particularly nasty nerve gas. It took less than an hour to kill 24,000 people and every animal inside the cordoned off area. They sent in clean up teams to remove the bodies, which were later buried in vast mass graves somewhere in the National Park. This happened a week ago, we think. Now you can appreciate why I said that we would like to turn the same weapons loose on the men who did such a despicable and cowardly act! But let me close on a positive note. Our leader D.R. has told me in confidence that a miraculous new protein has been discovered, and it appears to have amazing curative powers for the brain. It was discovered by a Japanese scientist and his American wife, but the discovery is top secret because some other properties of the protein have even greater possibilities for toppling the dictators all over the world soon. I can't say more than that now, but think about what good might come of a protein that could reverse the damage inflicted upon the Robotoids' brains. Would it be too much to hope that they might regain normalcy? No one knows for sure how many poor souls have been converted into Robotoids. We think that the three which you caught are a new breed. Most robotoids are used for industrial purposes and throughout the Mid-West and along the West Coast, there are Robotoids working in the manufacturing factories or as laborers in road gangs. But more disturbingly, we hear that the bodies of some Robotoids are used for sexual favours, even prostitution. Our agents have reported dozens of brothels have been opened in the Mid-West, to cater to the needs of the Army.   Imagine the Robotoid prostitute; a Robotoid makes the perfect whore: she or he never complains and will permit the client to do whatever they wish to their body, and will accept an endless stream of clients until they are physically worn out, or so diseased that their medical treatment bill exceeds the cost benefit to the employer. That whole concept is so disgusting!"

"Yes," Nick commented, "last night, once we realized that we could only get a response by ordering them to perform an action, we ordered them to take off their clothes so that they could shower. And then, they stripped naked, right there in front of us. The husband didn't seem to mind that we saw his wife naked and she even asked me if I wanted to have sex with her right away or after she had showered. Naturally, I put her straight. But the Robotoid behaviour is so alien to us, I'm sure that even the husband would have performed a sexual act for us if we had wanted it. It's so degrading that a human being should be reduced to such a state!"

David raised a question that had been bothering him too, "Doctor, I know that in their present state they are incapable of resisting any order. They are programmed that way psychologically and chemical pathways have been created in their brains that bypass the brain's normal decision centres. But my question is this; won't the memories of the actions that they have performed also surface? Certainly, they are incapable now of *resisting* by an act of the will, but the brain remembers what the body has done, and the more it repeats an action the greater the reinforcement to the memory centre of the brain. So, when your experts start the rehabilitation therapies, how will you deal with the suppressed feelings of guilt, anger, fear or despair that will emerge with the memories?"

"David, those are all valid points. And the honest answer is that we doctors just don't know what will happen to a reversed Robotoid. This is unexplored territory for the field of Medicine. Maybe the memories *will* drive them into madness or dissociative states that we cannot predict. But as doctors, we have to try. Otherwise, what is the alternative; shall we just put a bullet into their brains? If I'm right, there are somewhere between 50,000 and 100,000 Robotoids working in the Olympians' factories now. This is a massive problem to be dealt with when a therapy becomes available, and we can only hope that the patients don't recall the bad memories. We can hope that it will be like a patient recovering from a coma, often he has no knowledge of his state during his coma period. That would be a mercy actually, and the best outcome for all. But, like I said, we just don't know, and the human brain remains a miracle of creation to me."

Dr. Phillips led them through to a small private office so that they could talk. "Let me tell you that everything that is said in this regional HQ of the American Eagles is secure. I can vouch for my staff. Every one of them had lost close family members or suffered the personal loss of finances or careers as a result of the direct actions of the Regime before they joined us. They never leave this building. As far as the outside world is concerned, they have ceased to exist; in fact, this whole floor doesn't exist on any plans held by the government. We pay no bills, and the Regime pays for the utilities as part of the Central Hospital's bill! If the power should happen to go down, the hospital has backup generators and so we are better off than if we had an independent facility on the surface. The computer section screens all communications to and from the hospital also, so we monitor our security. But if there was ever a breach, we are all agreed that we will detonate explosive charges that will destroy this floor and the upper basement level. Everyone down here will die as martyrs to the cause of freedom. Oh, and we all carry a suicide pill, just in case we happen to be caught by a patrol on the surface, but since few of us do go out, it's a small risk. That is the level of our commitment, guys."

"Doctor, I have to admit, and I think this goes for Nick too, there was a time back there when we wondered whether we had blundered into an elaborate trap! But we believe you, don't worry about us. But I would also like you to know that everywhere we go, we are meeting people just like you and your team: totally loyal and dedicated, and ready to lay down their lives for this cause. Amazingly, there have been very few American Eagles captured, and those who were caught committed suicide rather than lead the Regime to their contacts in the movement. This is a life or death struggle for the whole Union. What has happened in small towns like Mitchell today will eventually come to the Americas' cities. It is heartening that a discovery like a new protein might be the ultimate weapon that will bring down the whole apparatus of oppression. I can't imagine what it does, and maybe its better that I don't know, if I don't need to know. I am sure that D.R. would have told me if he thought that I should know.

You had better issue us a suicide pill each too: the knowledge that we carry of the network and operations, as well as the key people that we meet; well, its invaluable information!"

"Yes, I agree." Dr. Phillips reached into his desk drawer and brought out a small red pill box. "I suggest that you keep the capsule within easy reach, or it can be implanted so that a blow to the spot will break it and the drug will enter the blood stream. Personally, I prefer the second option, I have mine concealed in my armpit. You have to hope that no one ever does a vigorous pat down on you though!" he joked. "Now shall we take a look at the Intel that you have gathered on your travels? We have lots of hardware available for editing and suchlike. I know that you, Nick, can do all of that and David will prepare the voiceovers. By the way, you'll love our new voice synthesizer gadget. You speak normally in one side and whatever voice you need to use will emerge from the other side of the system. We can program it to replace your voice with a particular speech pattern, like Ian Sharpe's, and it's true to every inflexion and uses his usual idiom. Wouldn't it be fun to have Sharpe doing the commentary for a documentary about his regime?" They all laughed, "And may I add that no one can unscramble the encoding of the synthesizing machine. There's not another like it anywhere, one of our geeks built it!" He said proudly. "Come, we'll demonstrate it.'

They went back into the operations room, and a young man was called over. Dr. John spoke quietly to him for a moment, and then he turned back to David and Nick. "Now you just listen to this." Presently, the young man began to speak into the machine via a lip mike. From the machine, a different voice emerged, and it was played through the public address system. Everyone stopped to listen; this was obviously a regular form of amusement. The voice of Ian Sharpe, complete with his characteristic hesitations, said, "Ladies and gentlemen of the American Eagles, I welcome you to my humble home. I just wanted to say what a terrific job you are all doing. I deserve to be punished, you know, I really have been a bad boy; a bad, bad boy, actually. So what you are doing is very patriotic and the sooner that you kick out the traitors from the government of the Americas, the better! Thank you all for your attention, and goodbye!"

The room erupted in cheers, shrill whistles and laughter, and the visitors joined in too. "So what do you think, David, can you use this for your propaganda? I can imagine what confusion this would sow in the regime's ranks. If you have enough computer power, the message could also be transmitted in other languages to that of the speaker; it only needs the databank to be loaded with plenty of sound bytes and the software can build a profile of the targetted output speaker. I will discuss with Duane about circulating the build specifications and copies of the software throughout the network."

The same young man approached Dr. John again and spoke to him privately. Dr. John nodded his head vigourously. "Good news again! Your presence has been catalytic, we are ready to commandeer some of the drones, and we will fly them to a secure location and examine their payload. If they are carrying explosives or nerve gas, then the American Eagles' controllers will send them against the regional command centre of the military commander. Who knows, we may even be able to drop a bomb on his head!" His face lit up with pure joy at the prospect. "Come over here to see the video being transmitted and recorded from the original drone that we captured."

They walked across to a large wall display panel where the live feed was showing a flight of four drones following the Big Sioux River. Suddenly the drone wingman peeled off from the formation and headed for the Grasslands Park. Immediately, the rest of the flight also scattered, and each drone was taken to a separate location. The video was broken for a minute or two, presumably while each drone was being checked. A text message flashed on the screen, it was from the ground team, and it said, "Alpha One team, High explosive charges found. Proceeding to execute Topcat!"

"We are switching to a video live feed now from the original drone," Dr. John explained, "Alpha One has indicated that we have bomblettes on board. These are basically anti-personnel weapons. I think that our operations controller will select an appropriate target. We are waiting for the other reports to come in, but we will be surprised if there is any cluster bomb units with gas loaded onto a routine drone patrol."

The display panel now showed a drone circling a military base which had an airstrip. There were lines of drones on the tarmac, and nearby some troops were lined up for an inspection by an officer. Along the foot of the screen, three more text messages had appeared, two of the drones carried anti-personnel bomblettes and air to ground rockets, while the fourth drone did indeed have nerve gas cluster bombs on board!

The controller gave orders for all of the drones to converge upon the base, and while drone number one dropped his payload on the soldiers standing on parade, drones number two and three took out the parked drones. Meanwhile, number four drone dropped its nerve gas payload of cluster bomb units directly upwind of the administration buildings.

The whole operation happened so fast, it was over within five minutes, and a pall of smoke drifted across the field. Men could be seen dropping like flies as the gas did its deadly work. The operations room was now deathly quiet as the video drone circled the base. One military vehicle made a break for it, heading for the main gate and the highway. No doubt that was the regional commander. The drone closed in on the vehicle. It was a regular staff car. Two air-to-ground rockets were fired from point blank range and the staff car somersaulted in flames, coming to rest on its roof with its wheels still spinning. The American Eagles controller ordered the drones to disperse, and they flew at tree top height to prearranged locations where crews would dismantle the drone aircraft. There was no jubilation in the American Eagles' operations centre. No one enjoyed the distasteful bloodletting that had just taken place. But the strike was a slap in the face to the Regime, serving notice that the end of their dominance had begun. The American people were taking their freedom back!

David asked Dr. John for a moment. He stepped away from the controller's desk and taking David by the elbow he steered him over to his office. "David, you look extremely upset, is there something wrong. Those men who died in that drone assault were accomplices to the genocide at Mitchell. Then they carted off a whole township to bury them like cattle which had been slaughtered in a foot and mouth outbreak. Don't feel sorry for them, they got what they deserved."

"Yes, I realize that and while I understand that it was necessary for the army to be taught a lesson that they would understand, I have never served in combat and to see men dropping like that rouses every decent instinct against it. But that wasn't why I asked for a word, I actually wanted to ask you about the Robotoids that we brought in, the Leasing family. What will become of them?''

"Well, we don't have the facilities or expertise to deprogram them here, even if it is possible with current medical technology. We shall have to treat them as we would a mental patient, but with this difference, our psychologist will be looking for the trigger words that were inserted in the induction programming. It's not simply a matter of injecting chemicals and then they will function as Robotoids, no, the injections must clean the slate prior to hypno-suggestion in order to insert sophisticated programming. But these bastards are getting lots of practice, and I'm certain that now they know exactly where to place the chemicals so that all moral code behavior is suppressed. I've even heard that the military is developing technology that will reprogram the mind to create immediately Robotoids with special skill sets, like pilots for example. Now we are in the realm of science fiction and it's frightening to me!''

"Yes, this science is taking us in a dangerous direction, and we have to put an end to it. The real monsters are not the Robotoids, but those who carry out these procedures; doctors like you who once took the Hippocratic Oath are actively participating in mutilation of healthy individuals. And do you know, Doctor John, this madness is being orchestrated by a bunch of Devil worshipers who have stolen our freedom!''

"Well, on the last point, I have no information, but I agree that certainly evil is present in the Union's institutions, we see evidence of that every day. Would you like to see the Leasing family, we have made them as comfortable as we can for now? They will remember you and Nick, and it might help them to settle down; my staff has told me that they are disoriented."

"Yes, why not?" David called Nick over and explained that they were going to see the Leasing family. Nick agreed and they followed Dr. John out of the operations area and up to the upper basement level where they housed resistance fighters and injured personnel. A special psyche ward had been hastily constructed but each patient had a personal room as well as a small communal area where they could sit together or have consultations with a doctor. Before entering Dr. John gave each of them a doctor's gown to wear, it might help, he explained.

The family was sitting in the communal area together when the trio entered the room. Bob Leasing and his wife, Amy, looked up when they entered and a flash of recognition came into their eyes. Jonathan didn't appear to be responsive; he sat looking at the holo-television panel which was inset in the wall. The screen was showing a cartoon for children.

Dr. John addressed the adults, "Bob and Amy, I have brought you some visitors. Do you remember them?"

Bob Leasing's attention returned to the screen, but he replied, "We gotta call in. The controller will be angry if we don't report in."

"I am David and this is Nick, Bob. Do you remember us, you came to our camper at Chamberlain."

"We gotta call in, " he repeated, "we gotta call in. We got to report the incident, you broke the rule, and you have to be punished. It's the law you know."

"Who says that it's wrong to help people?" Nick asked

"They say so, it's not allowed. We gotta call in. Where is my communicator, did you take it away?" Bob Leasing was becoming restless, he wrung his hands and he began to knock his knees together. Amy began to mirror his agitation, this was about to get out of control. Dr. John reached for the alarm button, but then David had a brainwave.

"We have new orders for you. First of all you have to relax." To his relief, they all stopped showing distress and young Jonathan Leasing also sat looking at them attentively. "This is your new instruction. You have been released from reporting in. We have decided that it is not wrong now for people to help you. The doctors and nurses here are going to help you, and you are to cooperate, and obey all of their instructions. You are also to give them a full history from the time that you left the hospital, do you understand? Answer me in the way that we taught you."

The three spoke as one, "we understand, we will obey your orders, Dr. Michael Roberts."

"Very well, sit together and watch the screen together. When the doctor or a nurse enters the room, you are to cooperate with them. We are leaving now. Be at rest."

The Leasings sat quietly, a faint smile on their lips, but they had switched off from their visitors and now watched the cartoons with rapt attention. Outside, Dr. John turned to David with amazement. "David, that was a brilliant idea! What made you think of that approach, we had been trying to find a way to get their cooperation, but without success until now."

"I dunno, it was just an inspired moment, I guess. Do you know the doctor that he mistook me for, this Dr. Michael Roberts"?

"I'm not sure. Let's go look him up in the database." They went back into his office and he started tapping keys on his console keyboard. A number of records flashed up on the screen. "Let's filter out the general practitioners and the vets, and those from outside this area. Chances are that this doctor is from this general area, if he is not military. Here we are, look at this guy. Dr. Michael Roberts, Clinical Psychiatrist, University of Chicago, and it gives a home address too. I think that Dr. Michael Roberts is going to have a house call. I'll have the Chicago brigade pick him up. That monster! We will put him to work in a constructive way, or if he refuses to cooperate we will persuade him." He picked up an empty syringe from his desk to illustrate his meaning. "It shouldn't be too hard to find him, unless he is out of town. But we have embedded agents in the military who can track him down if he is working in the FEMA detainee camps."

Chapter 3

It didn't take David and Nick more than three hours to edit and splice the video recordings taken from the backup data crystals on each of the drones. As it turned out, every drone was equipped with high resolution cameras and multi-spectral sensors for surveillance, so the material that was shown in the news flash was very professionally compiled. Using the American Eagles' technical know-how, they piggy-backed on the same military satellite which was used by the military for spying on the citizens of the Union. The film, which was five minutes in length, was broadcast in full holographic mode throughout the Americas. The broadcast interrupted the regular anemic programming with the shocking images of their military strike against the Regime of Ian Sharpe. Once again, Ian Sharpe's voice provided the commentary and extolled the bravery of the American Eagles freedom fighters, and also commended them for their bold initiative. The news flash continued with a prerecorded audio carrying an admission by Ian Sharpe of his crimes against humanity. Eventually the shocked network chiefs realised what was going out over their networks, and there was a nationwide shutdown of all holo-channels and radio broadcasting; but it was too late, much too late, because the cat was well and truly out of the bag by then!

The news was also being watched by Duane Richards, leader of the American Eagles resistance group. He was at his home in the Markham suburb of the Northside Dome in New Washington. His role in the resistance movement was a closely guarded secret and his identity was known only to a small circle of confidants. As a Supreme Court Justice, it had grieved him to see the Executive Branch of Government abuse its position and with the declaration of a State of Emergency back in 2052 under President Ben Tyler, the role of the Legislature and the officers of the two houses, and the Judiciary had ceased to hold any real meaning. The Freedom Party chose the Presidential succession, but in reality it was manipulated like everyone else by the Olympians. The Olympians were the ones who really ran the country, and they might be justly called an international criminal syndicate.

Duane knew all of these truths of course, and slowly and patiently, he had built up a cadre of like-minded men and women who felt the same way as he did. His second in command was James Duncan, a senior agent in the FBI. James, likewise, had found that within the Agency there were many agents that were repulsed by the criminal actions of the Freedom Party, but without an effective Judiciary and an elected Legislature, they were powerless to intervene. The Founding Fathers had foreseen the importance of the constitutional counterbalance.

The American Eagles was therefore a diverse group with but a single aim: to rid the Union of the Americas of the tyranny that had existed for forty five years. Every year, the resistance grew stronger, even as the Presidential dictatorship enacted its decrees for even greater curtailments of personal freedoms. So the resistance grew stronger and savvier about the use of guerrilla tactics against a well-armed and ruthless opponent: convoys carrying detainees were often attacked and the prisoners released; the state-controlled media was regularly hijacked to broadcast the propaganda of the resistance and denounce the criminal actions of the Freedom Party and the Olympians. But the news flash that Duane and James were now watching, together with three hundred million citizens of the Americas, gave them their greatest joy.

They clinked their glasses and toasted the Sioux Falls chapter of the American Eagles. "James, they actually did it! Imagine a surprise attack on the area command centre, and possibly they have eliminated the worse of the military collaborators in the process. That business at Mitchell really sickened me, you know. Dr. John tells me that our dynamic duo, David and Nick, have also got some footage from the Interstate which shows the deserted streets of Mitchell and scores of dead fish along the James River banks, and let's not forget the live ground video of the cleanup operation after they had gassed the herd of cattle, and the footage of citizens queuing in the streets for bread. That will make for compulsive viewing after this evening's show!"

"Well we can celebrate for the time being anyway. But what will be the response from the Regime? Surely they won't try to mount another operation like the Mitchell massacre?"

""Yes, they may try. The authors of that action may have been killed in the military strike which we have just watched; however, there are others in the Regime, who wouldn't hesitate to employ lethal gas against civilians if they wanted to. But the situation has changed, James, now we have the means to hit them before they can hit the city. They will be trying to prevent us from taking control of their drones again. I'm going to call John Phillips and ask him to hit the other military camps along I 90. Let's strike while the iron is hot. Every Municipal Airport has been put to use by the military. Our reconnaissance photography, which was taken from the military satellite when we hacked it, shows concentrations of men, weapons and equipment on all of those sites. In fact, it almost looks like a staging area for a war! If we can continue to override their air and ground controllers and hijack their military satellite, we may be able to steal more drones and weapon systems. I want those murderers to be so afraid every time they walk outside, or if they see a drone in the sky to think that it may be about to attack them. Last time we had the element of surprise and we caught them knapping. I fear that the next attempt will be harder if we follow the same tactics, so we need to keep shifting our focus."

"Yes, so let's think. Hmm, what does every army need: what about food and water? Let's cut off their supply lines. They will be forced to send out convoys under armed escort. Then we hit the fuel dumps and the tankers. We can isolate the garrisons and demoralize the troops. Then we attack the installations."

"Have we got the means yet to manufacture our own drones or obtain fresh weapons to arm them? I believe that we can build the drones in our Mid-West bases, using the same military design, but arms are a difficult issue because they are heavily protected, especially the Regime's stockpiles of nerve gas. Let's think about that problem and then we will make our suggestions to the area commanders."

"Yes, James, we'll think on it a while, but I still want to hit them all along I 90 before they can regroup and mount a counter-attack against the civilian populations. I will call John Phillips after supper to congratulate him and suggest widening our offensive. I also need to speak with David Mackintosh to discuss his return; he has been in the field now for three months and he and Nick need a break. But now it's time to eat! Bob, my household treasure has cooked us Beef Wellington tonight, which is my particular favourite;

followed by your favorite, crème brûleè. Bring your beer with you; it'll go well with the beef."

They walked through to the dining area where Bob had prepared yet another culinary delight. Bob was indeed a household treasure, and in spite of his advanced years, he still managed to create meals that delighted the palate.

After dinner, Duane placed a secure call to Dr. John Phillips. Dr. John was quietly confident that they would be able to press home their advantage. "Duane, I have been thinking about attacking the convoys of military trucks that are ferrying arms and ammunition up into the Dakotas. Interestingly, they avoid the Interstate Highways and, as much as possible, they travel under armed escort on the secondary highway system. I think that they are trying to avoid being caught out in the open on the I 90 and other main routes which cross the Badlands and the Grasslands. We can use this to our advantage, since we can hijack their military satellite whenever we wish, and our eye in the sky will monitor such convoys using its multi-spectral capabilities."

"That's great, John! I am most anxious to limit our risk of casualties or having our men captured in a counter attack. Do some reconnaissance of the routes. We will mine the bridges and other vulnerable points along the roads. But until we can rearm our drones, or commandeer some fresh ones, that option is closed I think. Still, thinking positively, I am sure that we shall be successful and then, as James and I agree, we need to cut the supply lines for food and water, hit their fuel supplies and reduce their stockpiles of weapons by massed aerial attacks. If you can capture some nerve gas, we will terrorize the Regime's forces, just as they have terrorized the civilian populations. But in all this, our center at Sioux Falls *must remain a secret.* Otherwise, they will do what they did so effectively at Mitchell. "

"Yes, Duane. It's understood. In fact we will draft in volunteers from North Dakota who know nothing of our facility, so in the event of capture, they will be unable to provide information that would lead the Regime to our doorstep."

"Thank you, John; it has been on my mind for a while, even before today's strike on the area command. Now, if I may, I would like a brief word with David."

"Sure thing, I will fetch him, but first I want to share something. The credit belongs to David actually, but we managed to discover from the Robotoid family, the name of the doctor who was responsible for their programming. We are going to pick him up and we shall interrogate him to discover how he did it, which key words he implanted and so forth. Thanks to David we now know how to reverse some of the programmed responses, but we shall learn even more when we have that monster in our hands. I keep you posted on that as it develops"

A moment or two later, David Mackintosh came on the line. "Hello, Duane, it's good to hear your voice after a long while."

"Yes, for me too. I wanted to congratulate you and Nick for the sterling job that you have been doing for the past three months. And you are also to be congratulated for unearthing the doctor who programs the Robotoids. This was just the breakthrough that we have been waiting for, well done! Also, the information that you and Nick have gathered and broadcasted has been first rate. Do you know that the Army desertions in the past three months have tripled the figure for the whole of last year? The propaganda war is proving a very effective weapon. Morale in the Army is at an all-time low and our raids on the payroll transfers only make it worse. We are winning this war, David. Soon we shall be entering the final phase and we have a secret weapon that we shall bring to bear that will be the decisive blow that will defeat Ian Sharpe, The Freedom Party and the Olympians as well. When you return I will brief you, but even on this secure line, I won't talk about this. Now, it's time that you both had a rest. Three months of stress will take its toll on any man, and you will be refreshed by a spell in Markham. Not only that, but you carry in your heads invaluable intelligence, too valuable to be in an active war zone, so I am recalling you now. Dr. John will make all of the arrangements."

"OK, whatever you say, Boss! But in the event of capture, we will not divulge any information. Dr. John has implanted capsules under our armpits that contain cyanide. We only need to break the capsules and death will be instantaneous, we are serious about this!"

"Well that is serious alright, and I have such a capsule myself. I didn't want to ask that of you. It's a big decision and it ought to be a personal one. Hopefully, this will all be over in a couple of years, or maybe less, and we can all have them removed. Go get some rest. You will be leaving early but you will be travelling light. Dr. John is sending your sensitive equipment separately so that it will not draw any curious notice at check points enroute. Keep your stills camera and the video camera with you, but the rest we will take care of. Take plenty of tourist photographs around Sioux Falls, play the part and look like normal tourists. We will supply you with supporting documents that will show that you have been staying at a small local guesthouse. Your camper will be relocated also.   Don't worry; we will get you a replacement for your next tour!"

The following morning, after they had toured the tourist sites about the city, Dr. John and the entire team came to see them off. In the brief visit they had all become good friends, and David and Nick's escapade across the heartlands had earned everyone's respect. A hospital car dropped them off at the central bus station where they were given tickets to travel south to Sioux City. There was a small airfield to the west of the city, called Martin Field.   A car was waiting to meet the Greyhound bus at Sioux City and it drove them out to the field. The airfield was a sleepy little facility and no longer in regular use by the military, so there were no formalities for their flight on the executive jet that was waiting for them. A sudden cold wind swept in from the north, and David shivered as he reached for his bag. He would be glad to leave these wide open spaces where men had died in obscurity, and met pointless and terrible deaths.

In as long as it took to transfer their cases to the cabin, they boarded and the jet taxied to take off. In minutes the area air traffic controller gave the clearance for the departure and they were able to take off. Soon they were cruising at forty thousand feet and looking down upon the vast cornfields along the Nebraska-Iowa State border; their filed flight plan stated that they were to overfly Omaha before heading to Kansas City, then east over St. Louis and on to New Washington.

"I guess they took the flight from Sioux City to avoid the air traffic around Sioux Falls. I can imagine that after yesterday's action the skies in that area must be buzzing with military traffic."

"Yes Nick, and in the circumstances, we were removed as quickly as possible. Duane was worried about the possibility of our capture, but I told him about the capsules. It turns out that he has one too, but he left the decision up to us. You know, he's the most decent man I know. He'd make a good president, you know? Well, we will see what the future will bring, but he said to me that this whole show will be over within two years; imagine that, after almost forty five years of dictators, we are finally going to be able to elect a real President, a Congress and a Senate and have Courts that will actually dispense justice! This is like a fairy tale, or I'm dreaming and one day I'll wake up and discover that is all it was."

"David, a man has gotta have a dream. But you don't have to be asleep to have a dream, my friend. Anyway, speaking of sleep, I'm going to recline this executive armchair and set the massage mechanism working and I shall sleep my way across half the country. Wake me when we reach New Washington, Pal."

The jet's flight plan had received clearance from the highest level and as officially it had been chartered by the Director of the FBI, no one questioned the pilot too much. As the plane flew into the patrol areas of different military commands, military fighters flew close by to check it out but soon departed satisfied. David was not as fortunate as Nick who had that uncanny ability to sleep in any situation, so his mind ran back on some of the events of their epic tour. He remembered those long queues for bread in the small Mid-western towns that they had driven through. Men, women and children shivered in the early morning dew, and they clutched their ration cards; it was hard to believe that such images had been filmed in the Union.

One expected that in a poor Third World country, but in America? Then there was that place outside Boise, Idaho that was being used to train Robotoids as shock troops.

They had stumbled upon the training camp by accident when they took a wrong turning while looking for an official camp site. The training camp was situated in a valley near the Craters of the Moon National Monument. Somehow they had missed the sign for the camp site, and as darkness was about to fall, they heard the sounds of shouting and gunfire coming from the valley below. Nick had his nice German telescope out in seconds and linked it to the video screen, and using the light intensifier they had captured the most amazing footage. There was a large body of men carrying weapons and they stood in lines at one end of the valley. It soon became obvious that they had been commanded to walk toward the head of the valley to storm a structure that looked like a blockhouse. At a command, by a blown whistle, the men began advancing toward the blockhouse, firing their weapons as they walked purposefully along the valley in a long transverse line. There were shots coming from the blockhouse too, but the valley floor had been mined and as the line of attackers kept walking the mines began exploding, but the attackers just kept walking forwards as if nothing had happened. As they watched the carnage, David and Nick continued to film. Over two hundred men were cut down by the withering fire coming from the blockhouse and the exploding antipersonnel mines; but the survivors continued to walk on, until eventually they reached the target and executed the remaining defenders. Only Robotoids could have persevered under such fire, no sane man would have even attempted to storm such a blockhouse by a frontal attack, passing through a minefield on the way. At the conclusion of the exercise, another whistle blew and open backed military vehicles appeared from behind the blockhouse, the bodies of the fallen Robotoids and defenders were collected and thrown into the backs of the trucks.

Were these the soldiers of the future? Were these the Olympians' shock troops? These were men who had been programmed to mindlessly walk toward certain death in order to subdue enemies. It was a chilling demonstration of man's inhumanity towards his fellow man.

As they had travelled east, they had witnessed more examples of Robotoids being exploited. Road gangs working in the midday sun, cracking rock with sledge hammers. If they fell from exhaustion, no one bothered with them: they could lie there until quitting time or die. The guards were indifferent either way.

They had also noticed the whorehouses in the vicinity of the military camps, the whores who were mainly women, usually stood outside in the streets wearing scanty clothes; they were picked over by men in uniform and taken inside the whorehouse. It was so demeaning and it had repulsed both Nick and David. David took a lot of still shots as they passed by, but they had to make a run for it once when a patrol spotted their camera.

This was the profession that David had chosen. It was still his life's blood, but it was hard to bear to see such things. Yet he felt that it was his calling to record these atrocities, to awaken the Americas to the evil that dwelt among them. If he remained silent, wasn't he acquiescing to the acts of these barbarians. It was this dilemma that had persuaded him to leave the sinecure of an anchor job at the All-American News Channel. The evidence of the regime being a police state was all about him: the spy bugs that constantly monitored the citizens, hidden microphones in elevators and on park benches to trap the unwary, tapped telephones and electronic bugs in his apartment in Toronto. No one could be blind to these intrusions and invasions of privacy. So, he had to do something in all conscience.

He wasn't an activist by nature, but when he learned of the existence of the Robotoids, it was also hard not to judge harshly the men who had perpetrated such a mutilation upon their fellow men and degraded them to mere automatons. It went against every decent bone in his body.

He thought some more about the Robotoids. He had seen them distantly on his travels, passed them in the streets and highways as they drove the Ventura, but that was impersonal. But actually meeting the Leasing family had made it so real to him. Talking with them, you could see that they were not mindless brutes and it was not their fault that they were as they had become. Others would have to answer for that hideous desecration of their humanity. Even though the small family unit had acted in a programmed manner, he wondered whether somewhere deep within their psyche, their humanity still survived. Or had the terrible work of the chemicals made irreversible the imprinting upon their minds? He hoped with all his heart that the Leasing family could be restored by Dr. John and his staff. That there might be a hundred thousand more of such persons trapped within a prison of the mind, brought an overwhelming sadness upon

David; he wept, for truly man's inhumanity to man knew no bounds.

Duane Richards sat at home alone, quietly watching the news channels, he was hoping that there might be some reports following up on the military strikes in South Dakota, but it was the usual inane coverage of unimportant local news which had returned to the holo-reporting. Bob had popped out to the local convenience store outside the cluster, and Duane had given the driver the night off. He sipped at his Coors, but somehow the drivel that was being spouted on the news just depressed him more, and his beer had gone flat. He was about to switch off the set, when suddenly across the screen there appeared some text. It was in a freehand scrawl over a background of light blue, it read, "You are being observed, turn off your set!"

Duane was shocked, this was so unexpected. Was he being observed through his own television? He had heard somewhere that it was possible. He walked across to the wall power outlet and switched it off. "Oh good, that's better!" said a man's voice behind him.

Duane turned around; a middle aged man sat comfortably reclining in one of Duane's favorite easy chairs. His clothing was unusual, long flowing robes which were white but also translucent. The manner of dress resembled somewhat that of a Bedouin prince or perhaps an image of Lawrence of Arabia that Duane had in his library. The stranger's hair was white, but it was largely concealed beneath a covering of the same material as his dress. His eyes were a bright blue, and rather startling in their intensity; there also seemed to be a sort of halo about his whole body. He smiled back at Duane as his eyes swept over the stranger.

"Are you an angel?" Duane asked. The question seemed somewhat foolish even to his own ears and it certainly amused his visitor.

"No, I'm not, I'm afraid. Left my wings at home, if I was! Allow me to introduce myself, Mr. President, my name is James Stewart, my friends call me Jim."

"Why did you address me as Mr. President?" Duane asked. "I'm a Supreme Court Justice. My name is Duane Richards and I have no involvement with politics, James."

"Yes, I know who you are. Well, forgive my mistake, Duane, got to get my facts right! Yes, you are Judge Richards in this era, but that will change. You are going to be the next President of the Americas. And to answer your next question, yes I sent the message to your screen. I have a handy little gadget that interfaces with all sorts of electronic equipment." He held up a small device, the size and shape of a golf ball. "Duane, please call me Jim. And please relax, I am a friend. I have come to see you for several reasons, and I have come a long way to do this. Yes, a very long way." Jim paused to consider his statement and a look of sadness flitted across his face.

"Jim, how did you get into my house? It is extremely secure against intruders and besides, friends usually knock you know, and they use the front door."

"Hmm, well perhaps they might if they wanted the persons spying on your house to know that you have received a visitor, but I thought it best to just drop in through the portal."

"Portal? Jim, you aren't making much sense to me. Which portal are you talking about? I see no portal in the ceiling of this room, and the windows and door are closed too. I don't wish to be inhospitable, but who are you, where did you come from and what do you want?"

Jim laughed, "All very reasonable questions, Judge. Let me begin by correcting your interrogation. It is not so much as 'where' did you come from, as 'when' did you come from? You see, I have come from the future, your future, about seven thousand years from now. But where I live there is no time, and space has no meaning. Something happened in the future. I had to make a choice in order to save my family, and in fact the whole world. It meant essentially giving up my flesh and blood, my human body, but not my humanity. I can move freely through time and space now, but I will never be the same as you again." Again the sad look flitted across his visitor's face.

Duane sat down on the edge of the sofa before he staggered and fell from the shock. "Jim, you say that you are from the future? I have to take your word for that of course. Tell me about yourself, please."

"OK," Jim replied easily, "I'll tell you what I can, but I don't want to give information that might destroy this timeline, so with that caveat, here goes. My name is Jim Stewart; I came from Priddy, in the County of Avon in England. I was a telecommunications and security expert acting for the British Government in security issues. You may have heard of Stewart Scanners?" Duane nodded his head, but said nothing.

Jim continued, "Yes, well at this moment, my other self of this era, is living and breathing right now in Priddy, with my wife, I have three very remarkable children by the way; and my two brothers and their wives live with Jim. Jim is unaware of my presence in this time epoch, and he doesn't need to know either. My three children are your hope for the destruction of the Freedom Party, Ian Sharpe and The Olympians. They carry the Kyoto Protocol in their genetic material. They are natural telepaths. You are discussing with other resistance groups worldwide how they might be used to bring down the dictatorships that are plaguing the world at the moment. I'm telling you this so that you can verify what I am telling you. I know that what I have already disclosed is very privileged information. Why not look me up on the web? There's sure to be an image of Jim Stewart, President of Stewart Scanners and Security Systems''.

"OK, I will, let's see if you are who you say you are. And if you are not, I am going to have to ask you to leave. Is that fair enough?'' Jim nodded and he had a slight smile on his lips. Duane crossed the room and powered up his console. Soon he was typing in his query and the image of Jim flashed up on the screen. It was a younger Jim to be sure, his hair was brown and the eyes didn't look so intensely blue, but it was Jim alright.

"Wow, is that one of the old technology computers? The other Jim has a quantum one, or he is about to obtain one, and it's so fast. His brother John is the whiz with it. Bill and I just plod along. Anyway, you will have a new one courtesy of Stewart brothers one of these days, if I can manage to manipulate them into it! I can't give you this one though, that would be crossing the line. So I guess you believe that I am who I said I was. Actually, I wasn't a bad looking chap in those days. No wonder my wife, Sakura, fell in love with me at first sight. We were together for seven thousand years you know? I miss her terribly, even now.''

Again the sad look came to his face for a moment, and then he refocused and said, ''Now look at your screen, I have isolated it from the Department of Homeland Security who were spying on you, so it's safe now. This device responds to my thoughts, quite clever isn't it? You will have all of these technologies too, but in a few more years. Now I want to begin with some information. Duane, this is *very important*. One of your close circle is about to betray you as the leader of the American Eagles. Do you know this woman? Elizabeth Fitzgerald isn't it?"

Elizabeth's face appeared on the holo-screen. "Now the next image shows her entering the Department of Homeland Security headquarters building, here in Annapolis, New Washington. She has gone there to seek an appointment with the new Director, David Roberts. He is also an Olympian by the way, and it might be a very good idea for you to kill him. David Roberts was too busy to see her on that day, which was Tuesday of last week, and his staff didn't realize that she was the real deal. But she has an appointment for the day after tomorrow. At that meeting, she intends to identify you as the leader of the American Eagles. Then you will be arrested and history will be irrevocably changed. I'm here to make sure that this does not happen. It's all about money, Duane. She needs an operation for her mother and she wants money for the hospital bills, pure and simple. I think that James Duncan ought to be told about this threat without delay. I have some other stuff to share, but they can wait."

Duane was visibly shaken by the disclosure. "Jim, are you sure about this. Why it's almost unbelievable! Elizabeth has been with us for ten years now. She has been one of our most trusted members of my inner circle. But definitely I will have James check it out; he has agents embedded at DHS with access to the Director's office 24/7." Duane picked up his comm. link and called James on the urgent setting. James answered on the second tone.

"Boss, has something important happened? Your face looks very tense."

"James, something *dreadful* has happened. We have a traitor in our core group. My source tells me that Elizabeth Fitzgerald has an appointment with the Director of the DHS, day after tomorrow. I am also informed that he is an Olympian. I have been told that it simply a question of getting money for her mother's operation. Can you confirm the appointment at the DHS? We should eliminate both her and David Roberts. My source is very reliable, and he will send you the corroborating images of her visit last Tuesday to the DHS." He looked at Jim for confirmation and Jim nodded and gave the thumbs up sign. "The images are on their way to you right now. Please call me back when you have a confirmation about the appointment."

James replied, "Wow, Liz, I can hardly believe it. I know that her health insurers were being difficult, but to do this? Why didn't she just ask one of us, I know that you wouldn't have turned her away? But you are right, once a person steps across that line, they can no longer be trusted again, and she knows a lot about us all! I will call you back in a few minutes."

Duane put down the comm. link and turned to Jim with a sad look on his face. "Jim do you want a stiff drink? If you don't, I do!"

"No, but thanks. Earth food and drink is just one of the sacrifices that I had to make when I made the change. I might nibble on a bit of angel food sometimes, but this body is pure energy, and I get all I need from the universal energy sources."

Duane shot him a doubtful look, this was getting weird. "How do I know that you are in fact from the future and can hop around in time and space?"

"Good question. Hang on for a moment!" In a flash Jim had disappeared only to reappear moments later with a large piece of rock in his hands. "Now, Duane, this here is a special piece of rock. It contains some minerals and trace elements that are not found anywhere on Earth, or the Moon for that matter. You can show it to any space scientist or geologist and just watch their jaws drop!"

"How did you do that, Jim, you just disappeared and reappeared in a flash? That's a good trick, it would come in very useful in these days, I can tell you."

"Duane, I have a special calling. So far as I know there's no one else like me. But let me get on, even for me time marches!" Jim reached inside his robe and withdrew a bag. It was made of a soft cloth, like chamois leather in texture. "Now, inside this bag are several spherical objects. These balls should be handled with the utmost care. They contain the most powerful explosive known to man seven thousand years from now. I had to obtain special permission to even bring these to you, because of the danger of misusing their power. Just one of these could destroy this whole superdome. All you need to do is squeeze the ball and then throw it, I'd suggest in a projectile mechanism, or else you will disappear with everything else in the explosion. I suggest that your targets ought to be The Freedom Party Headquarters, The DHS here in New Washington and Ian Sharpe's residence in Vancouver, which I hear is now habitable again. The fourth ball you can keep for The Olympians when you locate their Headquarters. These are only suggestions of course, but my history records that you did in fact destroy these first three targets and their absolute destruction struck great fear into the heart of the enemy. Duane, I want you to know that I am with the American Eagles in this fight. When they are brought down here, their power across the world will be shaken too and then KP will finish them off."

Duane's comm. link began to ring. It was James. "Your information is confirmed. We will strike tomorrow. I will come to see you later. Goodnight."

Duane turned to talk to Jim, but he had vanished again. "That's an annoying habit, Jim," he muttered.

Chapter 4

The Department of Homeland Security (DHS) is the third largest department of the cabinet departments of the Union of the Americas following the alleged terrorist attack upon the USA which occurred on September 11th, 2001. At its formation the DHS was the third largest in the cabinet and in the past one hundred years the number of employees had risen to over a quarter of a million personnel. Its primary responsibility remained the same: to protect the Union of the Americas and its Territories and Protectorates from terrorist attacks, man-made accidents, and natural disasters and to initiate the proper response to any of these. The role of the DHS was most similar to the Interior ministries of other countries. Until the Declaration of Emergency Powers in 2052, the budget of the DHS was known, but at the time of writing of this journal, it had not been declared for some while, but some estimates for the current year stated that it was close to $125 billion. The headquarters for this megalithic department occupied the whole of the former St. Elizabeth's Hospital campus in Anacostia, in Southeast New Washington, D.C. The site accommodated over sixty former Washington-area offices into a single headquarters complex of almost 600, 000 square feet of administrative space.

The DHS complex consisted of a tall central tower which housed the Administration Department, the Director's Office and several floors devoted to the surveillance of the citizens of the Union of the Americas. This information was stored in a data processing facility which received real time updates from all the DHS regional centres. It was a vital facility and there was a twenty four hour military guard that ringed the building and patrolled the whole of the complex. The other departments were clustered around the Administration Tower in a pentagonal shape.

It took almost a day for the DHS Director to learn that Elizabeth Fitzgerald had an appointment with him, with the stated reason being that she wished to disclose vital information about The American Eagles' leadership and operations, in return for a sizeable payment.

David Roberts had only very recently inherited the post of Robert Montague. Director Montague had been removed from his office, by Ian Sharpe, owing to his incompetence in protecting the President Designate from assassination in Boston. Roberts had no intention of following in his predecessor's footsteps. Montague had been converted into a Robotoid and he could now be seen pushing a broom along the corridors of the New White House, with a vacant expression on his face. When Director Roberts heard that the front office reception clerks had failed to appreciate the importance of the visit by Elizabeth Fitzgerald, he immediately ordered the arrest of the entire reception team, pending a thorough investigation into the matter. All subsequent attempts to contact Ms. Fitzgerald had failed, but he ordered his staff to keep trying. Meanwhile, his aides ran a database check to find out about the lady, but strangely her name didn't appear in any government records. In a way, this confirmed that she must be the genuine article, and David Roberts looked forward to his meeting with her on Tuesday with great anticipation. This could be the break that he had been waiting for!

Elizabeth Fitzgerald lived in an old property overlooking the Suitland Parkway. Since her mother had entered the nursing home, she lived alone and had no close friends. Her work for the American Eagles had been her passion, until her mother contracted cancel of the bowel. An operation was urgent, but the insurance company had refused her application, claiming that her mother's cancer was a pre-existing condition, which was untrue. Her apartment block had been new at the time of the Big Ones and like all of the properties in District Heights, in Forestville, it had emerged unscathed from the disastrous tidal waves of 2050. But the neighborhood was now rundown, but it was all she could afford on her pension.

The team sent by James Duncan was commanded by Rick Blake, and they were all military Special Forces. After explaining the reason for the assassination, James had asked only two things, no innocent persons were to be harmed and her death should be quick, and preferably it ought to appear as an accident. He hoped that Elizabeth's mother might benefit from the life insurance.

On Monday morning, Elizabeth emerged from her building, and walked down the hill towards the commuter terminal. It was a wet and windy morning and she was struggling with her umbrella against the gusts of wind, so perhaps her attention was not as it ought to have been. The wind blew the leaves from the trees about and she squinted to see clearly. The truck which hit her had been stolen, it also had no brakes and mounted the sidewalk halfway down the hill and pinned her body against the trunk of a tree; her body lay like a rag doll beneath the truck's front fender; the driver disappeared after the accident. A witness to the accident said that the driver had hopped on to a dirt bike that had been following the truck. When the ambulance arrived, the medics pronounced her as already dead from massive trauma and her body was taken to the nearest hospital, which was in Suitland.

James called Duane with the news, "Duane, it is done. As a precaution, when you informed me about her, I had all of her data expunged from the government databases. There is no lead for Roberts to follow up and he will have to drop the matter."

"That's good, James. She was never the easiest person to deal with, and she was very independently minded. Perhaps that is why she wouldn't ask for help; too proud, I guess. Very unfortunate to have to kill one of our own, but we both agreed that it was very necessary. But let us draw something positive from this, it was a timely warning. We will have to pay much more attention to internal security to prevent a repeat of this sort of situation. I won't lose any sleep over the death of any traitor! But I am concerned for the mother. We will pay for the operation and her after care, but anonymously. Now we have much to talk over, James, apart from this affair. In fact, why don't you come over for lunch? There is something important that I need to show you and a wild tale to tell you too! Let's put this unfortunate business behind us."

"A wild tale, now that's intriguing! You have really stimulated my appetite, on both counts. I have been eating takeaways a lot lately; Bob's cooking will be a holiday for me."

Thirty minutes later a hybrid-engine taxi pulled up at the security gate of the cluster. James showed his ID and the guard called the residence for clearance. A few moments later, after a snapping off a crisp salute, the guard waved them through. The taxi driver was suitably impressed, "Gee, Mac, you must be *somebody*! The last fare I brought here had to get out and walk the last part; they don't usually allow taxis inside here." James merely smiled and gave him a generous tip, to reinforce that impression.

Bob had the door open, even before the taxi drew up at the entrance pathway. "Welcome, Sir. His Honor is expecting you. He tells me that you've been on hardship rations, but don't worry, Mr. James, there are T-bones on the grill! And your favorite dessert to follow."

James laughed and hugged the old retainer, "Bob, you are a life saver. Is the Judge in the living room?"

"No, Sir, he's in the den. He said for you to go right through when you arrive."

James found Duane looking intently at a large piece of black rock when he entered. It had a crystalline appearance, but it was otherwise unremarkable, and James wondered why Duane was studying it so closely. "Hi, Boss," he said by way of greeting, "what's with the rock?"

"Yes, indeed. What do you think of my rock, James?" he replied. "It looks quite ordinary to me, but then, I'm no geologist. But the guys at the Smithsonian are jumping over the moon about it. I sent them a piece off this lump. Do you know that there is probably not another piece like it anywhere on Earth?"

"Nah! You're pulling my leg, Duane. What's so special about this rock?"

"What's so special is that I meant it literally when I said, not another piece like it anywhere on Earth. This is extraterrestrial and it didn't come from a meteorite or an asteroid. Quite where it did come from, I don't know, but it was delivered to me here in my living room, actually by a man who popped out to get it."

"No, now I know that you are teasing me! If it is extraterrestrial, how could someone just pop out to get it? Stop teasing me, Duane."

"Well, the gentleman who brought me the rock told me that it contains elements and minerals that are not found on Earth. He gave it to me as evidence of his bona fides. And incidentally, he was the source for the Elizabeth Fitzgerald betrayal. I will tell you more about my visitor, but we shall speak over lunch, as you are in dire need of some good food, and T-bones are best when they are fresh off the grill. Come on!" Duane stepped briskly toward the door and James was a half pace behind him.

Bob had prepared two huge 20 ounce T-bone steaks, garnished with fried eggs and grilled tomatoes and a mushroom sauce. James was speechless and humbly knelt before the maestro. "Anytime, Bob, that this guy gets tired of your cooking, you just come to me. I'll even double your wages!" They all laughed, and Bob returned the obeisance with a mock half bow.

It took a while to get through the steaks, which were, as usual, perfectly cooked to each man's taste. Finally, James laid down his cutlery and leaned back in his chair to enjoy the wholesome meal. Duane finished soon after, and they rested for a while. They sipped their beers and enjoyed that warm glow that you get from eating a culinary delight. Then James returned to the earlier topic. "Please continue, Duane, with your story about the mysterious visitor."

"Very well then, I will. This is the 'wild tale' that I mentioned when you called me earlier. Simply put, a man in a white flowing gown suddenly appeared in my living room. He had first of all interfaced with my holo-television to send a warning that my screen was being accessed by the DHS. Once I had switched off the set, he appeared, as relaxed as you like. He was reclining in the chair that you customarily use. He carried a small device like a golf ball, and by merely thinking a command he was able to interface with it to control any electronic device, as he said.

First up, I asked him if he was an angel. He laughed at that and said that if he was, he had forgotten to pack his wings. He spoke with a sort of British accent, but provincial. He said that his name was James Stewart, but everyone called him Jim. He explained that he was from the future, but his persona was living during this time in England, in the County of Avon, which is in the south west part of the country. He said that Jim Stewart lives in Priddy, with his wife and three children, plus his two brothers and their wives. Now, here's something else that gives his story credibility. First of all, I looked him up on the web; the photo of Jim Stewart that I found was of a man in his early forties. But it was the same person, and this man was as fit and spry as a young man, but I sensed that he was very, very old. According to the official bio-data, Jim Stewart and his brothers run Stewart Scanners and Security, which are the most common equipment used in all security systems, worldwide. Secondly, he mentioned his three children who are the world's only natural telepaths. James, these children are our best hope for mankind, and their existence is a very closely guarded secret. We leaders of the resistance groups are planning to use them to bring down the dictators, at the next World Congress. How could he know these things, unless he is Jim Stewart, but from the future, and also he knows these things because to him they are recorded history!"

"So, we are supposed to swallow this tale on the basis of these facts? Duane, given enough resources,

74

anyone might have discovered Elizabeth Fitzgerald's treachery and the same is true of the telepathic children. No, I need more than this to persuade me, Duane, I'm sorry."

Duane merely smiled and got up from the table. "I thought that you might say that. I left the best for last, like your creme brûlée, which Bob is bringing through now. Enjoy yours, while I bring the final proof for you." James ate his brûlée with relish and Duane returned to the table.

"James, there are several devices inside this bag, they are from the future, seven or eight thousand years, I forget which. They are each powerful explosive devices. All you need to do is to squeeze one and then throw it, or as Jim suggested fire it with a projector because just one of these could destroy this whole dome''. He reached inside the bag and withdrew a small ball, about the size of a ping pong ball. He handled it with care and placed it without squeezing it on the tabletop. "James, my boy, you are to have the honor of flattening the Department of Homeland Security, and hopefully, vaporizing the entire establishment with its new director. After that we will destroy Ian Sharpe's new residence in Vancouver, quickly followed by the headquarters of the Freedom Party in Houston. Jim says that these targets appear in his timeline historical records, so I have no doubt you will succeed."

"Alright, given that what you say is true, the proof of the pudding is in the eating. So, we will drop one of these little balls on the DHS HQ. Nothing ventured, nothing gained, and we lose nothing by trying, correct? But rather than using a device to throw it, I propose that we drop it from a model plane, like the time that we gassed Ian Sharpe's residence. A projectile launcher would be too suspicious to tote it in a public place, and if it misfired, lethal for the operator and anyone else nearby. Jonas will do this job for us, his models are so dependable and if it began its flight in the air above a park, who would think twice about a model plane?"

"Very good, James. Now, did you leave *any* crème brûlée for me? No, I thought not! But fortunately, I too have a backup. Bob! He's finished it, bring out my dish please." Bob appeared beaming and carrying a small dish for Duane.

That Tuesday morning was the appointed day for the interview with Elizabeth Fitzgerald, so Director Roberts was hopefully awaiting her arrival, at or before ten o'clock. He had instructed the front desk to be on the lookout for the lady and to show her up to his office without any delay. It was a clear, cloudless sky, the rain had all cleared up and the sun was shining. "A good omen for me! The forecast is for fine weather all the rest of the day, certainly there will be no inclement weather that might dissuade her from coming down to Annapolis."

Jonas Parker had completed the pre-flight checks and his pride and joy model plane was ready to fly. He had selected Truxton Park as his launch point; along the east side of the park there is a little used road, called Primrose Road. It runs northward until the park's boundary with Spa Creek and it is only a short flight across the creek at that point, passing over some residential areas and then nearby is the site of the DHS headquarters complex. At that hour there were few people in the park; just some small children who played on the swings while their mothers or nannies watched over them. No one took any notice of Jonas as he started up his model plane and sent it off over the waters of Spa Creek. Jonas' model had a longer range than most model aircraft, because he had stripped out all non-essential materials to maximize its range. As instructed, he had carefully ensured that he left no fingerprints or genetic traces anywhere on the fuselage or engine components: it was as clean as it was possible to make it.

He launched the plane at 9:30 a.m. to ensure that it would reach its destination by 10:00 which was the designated time for the explosion. The plane was fitted with a wide angle lens camera with a link to his location. He had his video record playing from the take-off until the drop. James had been most explicit in his warnings about handling the small explosive device. Under no circumstances was he to squeeze the ball until just before takeoff and then the plane should make a smooth takeoff from a hard surface. Jonas could hardly believe that such a small object could be so powerful, but he had known James from childhood, and James never exaggerated, never.

So Jonas had decided to launch from the north end of Primrose Road. They had debated about the best altitude for the flight and decided that 1,000 feet would be high enough, rising to 1,500 feet above the DHS headquarters building. Jonas figured that his plane would be clear of the blast by the time that the bomb hit the ground and he was aiming to place the bomb right at the entrance of the tall Admin tower so that with a bit of luck the adjacent buildings also might be struck by falling debris.

Everything went smoothly. At that altitude, even the spy bugs were below him and the patrol area for security zones would be focussed on the Naval Academy and other military installations in the Annapolis area. The image of the towering administration block of the DHS showed clearly in his video display; it dominated the site, and it was hard to confuse the target. Jonas needed no trial approach run. He verified only the model plane's altitude, the altimetry meters confirmed that it was 1,500 feet and it was a wind-less morning. Jonas had been practicing the bombing run in his local park, and in just the same way he pressed the release control at the exact moment required. The model's bomb doors flipped open and the bomb fell free. He flipped the plane so that it would make a circuit of the site at a safe distance and directed the servo motor on the camera to point at the DHS Administration Tower at the moment of impact.

If he had had any doubts about the bomb before, the doubts evaporated just like the DHS headquarters buildings. There was a blinding flash, a deep booming noise which was followed by a huge mushroom cloud. As the model plane relayed these images to the American Eagles, the technicians linked them to a live broadcast feed and the images were displayed across the nation. When the dust began to settle, there was nothing to be seen at ground zero. Everything within a five hundred yard radius had been destroyed; at the center of the blast area, the buildings were simply vaporized. Jonas turned his plane around and keeping it low, he brought it back over the Spa Creek to Truxton Park. Within a short while he had dismantled the model and his plane was safely stowed in the back of his van. Jonas drove south until he met Hilltop Lane and then turned west for New Washington.

James and Duane were watching the operation together in Duane's residence in Markham. They were jubilant, having seen it twice, first on a link to the broadcast center and then as it was rebroadcast continuously across the networks to the whole nation with an audio commentary. "We certainly sent a message to Ian Sharpe today, Duane. And your mystery visitor has definitely proven his worth. I wonder why did he choose to help us?"

Duane hesitated before replying. "There may be a reason, but please don't repeat this to anyone, promise?" James nodded, his curiosity now aroused. "At the beginning of our conversation, he greeted me as Mr. President. I pointed out to him his error, of course, and he said a curious thing. Something like, 'Oh, my mistake! I must have got my time line mixed. You are *going to be the next President of the Union of the Americas.*' I believe that the Elizabeth Fitzgerald affair was his main reason. If I was betrayed, then the future would have been changed, he came to make sure that it wasn't. The star rock and the explosives were really incidental, evidences you might say, and not time line sensitive. We would probably have found a way to destroy these targets with conventional weapons at some future date, but this event today is epochal. We have struck fear into their hearts by displaying some awesome power that they can't explain: they don't know how it was delivered or what it was; I'm betting that it was not nuclear and there will be no radiation traces. No, the fear of the unknown is a mighty weapon, James!"

"Of course you are right about the weapon, and I will keep quiet about the Presidential election too, but maybe he is right. I can't think of a better man for the job, actually!"

At that precise moment the current President was vomiting his breakfast down the toilet in the attached bathroom suite of the Private Office in the New White House. Having seen the awesome explosion at

Annapolis, first on the American Eagles' broadcast and then later when the network news channels got their helicopters in the air, there was saturation coverage of ground zero. The news anchors were publicly speculating about the authors of the explosion, disregarding the censors. This story was just too big to suppress. Ian Sharpe was only brave when he had the upper hand, but fear like a knife stabbed him, each time that the news channels rewound the shots of the devastation. After Ian Sharpe had seen the multiple close-ups of the DHS site, his stomach reacted involuntarily and he began to vomit, he also urinated in his pants from the fear. He had no doubt that he was the next target and he had seen how ineffective the military guards had been. Fortunately, he always kept a clean change of clothes in the bathroom, and he was able to clean himself up before his aide entered.

"Mr. President, do you have any instructions concerning the Annapolis terror attack?"

"No, but get the Joint Chiefs of Staff immediately. I will meet them in my briefing room. I want to find out what happened before I make any public statements." The aide rushed out to summon the generals to the New White House.

Chapter 5

The long table of the President's briefing room had seen the end of many careers, particularly in times of crisis. No President wanted to be told that his elite cabinet or Joint Chiefs of Staff didn't have a clue about a pressing issue, and heads were apt to roll. The most likely fall guy wasn't there today, having been vaporized along with his entire staff and five thousand others who worked in the DHS headquarters complex. So, as might be expected, the late Director David Roberts was blamed for the whole incident. This didn't please Ian Sharpe one bit, because quite reasonably he feared that he might next on the chopping block, no, he wanted answers.

"General Browning, tell me what you know. And don't tell me 'I don't know', what was this device that was exploded, and how was it delivered will do for starters."

General Arthur Browning was a five star general and but he was not ambitious. He was responsible for overseeing the development of new weapons; in short he was a scientist in a military uniform, a science nerd and a bit immature for his position. Browning's appointment to the Joint Chiefs was recognition of his undoubted scientific genius, with a little helping hand from the very ambitious General Fraser who rode on his coat tails.

"Mr. President, it is too early to give you positive answers, but some negatives will help in this case too. My people rushed to ground zero, and we can confirm that it was definitely not a nuclear device, only background radiation is present which is to be expected after such an explosion. Secondly, no missile delivered the bomb. Our surveillance is extremely extensive in this sensitive military area and we are certain of this. Thirdly, there have been no reports of ground-based terrorists. Counter-intelligence reports no hints of terrorist activity, however, some sources have recently reported that the main terrorist threat, the so-called American Eagles may have developed a completely new weapon. We have verified that none of our space vehicles have been compromised, and no other country has an operational space -mounted weapon. The Russian Federation is said to be experimenting with a space-mounted exploration tool, or SMET, which is simply a very powerful laser array that can be focused on a single point with some accuracy. However, they have been having problems in maintaining the stability of that tool, so it is still not functioning accurately enough to pick out a target with such precision. In any case, this has all the hallmarks of an explosion at ground level, which is quite different to the SMET. The debris field indicates a single impact point and there are radial markers to support this conclusion also."

"So is that it? It's not the SMET; it's neither a conventional bomb nor a missile with a nuclear warhead. Then is there no defense against this weapon, and where may we expect them to strike next? General Fraser, give me your best shot."

"Then, if I had to guess, Sir, I'd say they will hit a military target next. They have effectively silenced the HQ of the DHS, and remember when they attacked before; they targeted the DHS offices in Boston and Chicago. They have been making a statement in my opinion. They wanted to emasculate the surveillance program over the civilian population. Since they have done that, I'm betting that they will try to hit a military site, probably a critical one. I recommend heightened security in all military zones. If they have found a way to evade the radar coverage, then we need more drones in the air, so that we can intercept their drone that is carrying this weapon. I don't think that we can consider any other strategy without knowing more about the delivery vehicle and the weapon, Sir."

"Yes, that sounds more like a plan to me. Please raise the military preparedness level. General Browning, I presume that your scientists are scouring the site looking for forensic clues, even as we speak?"

"Indeed, Mr. President. We hope to recover trace elements that will tell us the nature of the explosive. Probably they have discovered a way to boost the power of an existing formula."

"'Good, when do you expect to have some answers?"

"Give me a week. It's a huge area and it needs skilled technicians to investigate. I'm bringing in more staff from the West Coast and Mid-West, plus we have the FBI assisting us already. "

"OK, then that will be all for now, gentlemen."

The generals exited the room as quickly as possible. Several of them mopped their brows. Ian Sharpe was renowned for his ruthlessness and having the former Director of the DHS mopping the floors in the New White House was a salutary reminder of the price of failure.

Ian Sharpe felt somewhat better after the discussion, because as Browning had said, the negatives in their findings to date ruled out certain worrying possibilities, thank God that the American Eagles hadn't gone nuclear. He felt that this might be a good time to go to his bolt hole in Vancouver, Browning needed a week and there was nothing so pressing at the moment. His aide entered in answer to his summons.

"Jackson, make ready Air force One, I am going to Vancouver for a few days. Tell them to triple the security around the perimeter. These days anything is possible."

The President's comm. link began to ring. His aide, Jackson, answered it, he listened and asked the caller to repeat the message; his face went ashen. He turned to the President, who stood with a questioning look on his face. "Sir, your residence, it has been destroyed. It's just like the Annapolis bombing. There is nothing there anymore, just a very deep hole in the ground!"

After the meeting in the New White House, General Fraser immediately circulated an instruction to his Regional Commanders. Uncharacteristically, he had stuck his neck out, by betting on the next target of the American Eagles. In truth, no one had a clear idea where they might strike next. His analysts could only say that they appeared to be targeting the emblems of the Regime, which was a rather obvious conclusion anyway. Fraser didn't believe that they would continue with this policy, and he fully expected them to start making demands of a political nature soon. To his way of thinking, his best guess was actually a logical one, because the opposition would probably seek to show that they could defeat the Armed Forces by waging a guerrilla war, until a certain point when they would openly confront them. This had always been the pattern of guerrilla campaigns, but Fraser consoled himself that he held the edge in technology and weaponry.

His comm. link rang; it was his intelligence officer Colonel McKinney, or Big Mac as he was nicknamed, "General, I hope that you are sitting down? There has been another bombing. It looks just like the Annapolis attack. It has all the hallmarks of the American Eagles; they seem to be attacking the public face of the Regime. The target? It was President Sharpe's Vancouver residence, never did like that monstrosity anyway, but it's gone. It was just blown away. I have seen aerial coverage by one of our drones that happened to be in the area on a routine patrol. No, we didn't see any unusual activity in the area prior to the explosion. We lost two squads of Marine Guards who were all around the perimeter, plus five who were inside the residence. I have ordered a news blackout, but the news hovers are all over the scene, this story is bound to get out, if not on the holo-channels then it will be on the Web within minutes.''

General Fraser hung up. This bombing made it even worse. Sharpe would certainly take this very personally. The American Eagles were upping the ante now. It was as if they were openly defying the military to take them on. Well, if it came to an open confrontation, he had two choices: nerve gas dropped from drones or a mass frontal attack using Robotoids. He preferred the latter. The Robotoids just kept advancing; they were in many ways a military commander's dream soldiers. They were utterly incapable of fear and even when their comrades fell left and right, they would not shrink back. Yes, he rather relished the thought. Perhaps he could devise a plan to sucker the American Eagles into an ambush. He'd give it some thought. He also thought about which might be the first military targets; they would most likely go for a big splash. Andrews Air Force base seemed a likely candidate, but it was too near to Annapolis, they had tended to spread their activities across the continental Americas. Perhaps they had no forces in Hawaii or Puerto Rica? He rejected West Point Academy for the same reasons. Wherever they struck, he was confident that he had enough drones patrolling the skies to catch their carrier. He only needed to get his hands on one weapon, and then General Browning's boffins could discover the secret of the fearsome new explosive. He reviewed his stockpile inventory, yes; they had more than 50,000 drones in serviceable condition, which was more than enough.

In actual fact, General Fraser was dead wrong in his assessment as the American Eagles were at that very moment planning to dispatch another model plane over Houston; the target was the Freedom Party Headquarters. At the north side of the massive multilevel freeway intersection of Katy Freeway and the North Freeway, HOV there was extensive parkland called White Oak Park. The south east corner of the park was segmented by two roads, Houston Avenue and White Oak Drive. The Freedom Party had acquired the whole of the area bounded by these major roads and in the centre of it they had erected a sprawling and grandiose structure. The whole structure was clad in black granite, and it gave the building a somewhat imposing and some would say, a sinister aspect. From the roof of the building a huge flag of the Union of the Americas flew alongside an equally large flag of the Freedom Party. The message was clear; the two were indissoluble.

One week after the Annapolis bombing a small model plane was launched from the picnic area adjacent to the river which runs through White Oak Park. The protection about the complex was principally at ground level, but two Police hovers had been assigned to make periodic fly pasts every half hour. The Freedom Party Headquarters was not considered to be a primary target, but to placate the still irate Ian Sharpe, Fraser had put additional security on the site. The American Eagles' operatives monitored the security timetables and they found that the hovers' patrol routine was unchanging.

On Tuesday, at seven o'clock in the evening, the plane was launched. Once again, the result was a massive explosion followed by a huge mushroom cloud. The shock waves travelled across the whole city of Houston. When the dust had settled, once again there remained only a very deep crater, and the pride of the Freedom Party and its whole administration was vaporized in the heat of the explosion.

The news was instantly relayed to Ian Sharpe who was forced to reside now at the New White House. His aides rushed to tell him the news. He was sitting down to dine alone, in his private quarters, but they did not dare to withhold the news. His meal that evening was a meatloaf, prepared by his personal chef. As his aides burst through the door, he had just taken his first mouthful and was just savoring the taste; however the dramatic entry of his aides caused him to almost choke on the food. "What is the meaning of this?" he demanded.

"Sir, there has been another bombing. It was Houston, The Freedom Party Headquarters, it has gone Mr. President! It's vanished, vaporized, just like in the last two bombings." Jackson added, somewhat unnecessarily.

Sharpe rounded on him angrily, "No, that's impossible! I was told that the security forces were protecting the building with constant patrols. And what about the Executive, they were supposed to be meeting there at seven o'clock this evening?" Jackson shook his head sadly. "What everybody, all gone?" Sharpe sagged in his chair; this was a blow of unimaginable seriousness. This was nothing short of a disaster! How would he manage alone? After a few minutes, he rallied himself. "Get me General Fraser and General Browning. Let them come to me here." His aides rushed out of the room to carry out his command.

One hour later, and Ian Sharpe had thoroughly collected his thoughts and an icy calm sat on him. There was a knock at the door and the two officers were shown in. "So, Gentlemen, I suppose that you have heard of the latest outrage? What do you have to say? General Fraser, you go first. You said that the next strike would be a military target and I understand that you have deployed thousands of drones and hovers to protect the military establishments that you assessed as primary targets. Obviously you were incorrect. May I ask what resources were deployed to protect the Freedom Party Headquarters?"

"Sir, we had two hundred elite special forces monitoring the site. We had a mobile radar unit and listening equipment stationed within the site and security inside the building and on the roof. In addition, we had regular patrols by hovers, every thirty minutes. We saw nothing, but a few seconds before the detonation of the device, there was a small model plane observed, it was at an altitude of twelve hundred feet and it came from the White Oak Park area, Sir. The defenders didn't think that it constituted a threat."

"Are you seriously telling me that with all our rings of elite troops, radar and listening devices, not to mention observers posted on the roof, we were defeated by a model airplane that just waltzed through our elaborate defenses? That is unbelievable, General Fraser!" General Fraser was clearly embarrassed and he blushed a bright crimson, but offered no further words.

"General Browning, you asked for a week. You've had a week. What is your report?"

"Sir, we examined forensic clues at the Annapolis and Vancouver bombings. We did find some residue on the walls of the craters, and frankly, Mr. President, we are baffled. The residue contained unknown elements, never been seen anywhere on Earth before. The origin of these chemicals is unknown."

"So little green men dropped a bomb on my house, the DHS headquarters and presumably on the Freedom Party Headquarters too? Is that the best that you can do? Perhaps you would both benefit from a visit to the funny farm?" he remarked sarcastically.

"No, we wouldn't." General Fraser replied testily, "And the Joint Chiefs of Staff are wondering whether you are really up to the job, Mr. President? So far your leadership has been less than inspiring! We are tired of being treated by you as if we are a group of morons. We are taking over. I hope that you have enjoyed your meal? Anyway, the food in Leavenworth Prison will not be to your liking, of that I am sure."

General Browning walked over to the door and motioned to a detachment of Marines who were waiting in the anteroom. They marched smartly inside. "Sergeant at Arms, place this man in restraints. He is under arrest for treason against the Union of the Americas. He is to be taken in Air Force One directly to Leavenworth Maximum Security Prison to await trial. You will report to Colonel Brandon Wilkes at Andrews Air Base. He has everything arranged. If this man attempts to converse with you, or to countermand my orders, you have my permission to gag him. Is this clear? Here is a written copy of your orders, co-signed by every member of the Joint Chiefs. The Presidential Guard will cooperate with you; it has all been arranged with the commander."

Ian Sharpe protested, "Generals Fraser and Browning are you quite out of your minds? I am the President. You can't arrest me. You have no right! Release me immediately." He addressed the Sergeant at Arms, who was now placing plastic handcuffs on his wrists.

The Sergeant at Arms, addressed him directly, "Look, you heard my orders. You aren't the President now; you're just another prisoner, with a number. And we are under Martial Law. So keep your trap shut or I will gag you! Do you understand?"

Sharpe looked at him with shock and disbelief, but as the new reality sunk in, a tear rolled down his cheek and he nodded silently. "Take this garbage out of my sight!" General Fraser ordered. He walked across to the table, where a large piece of meatloaf was untouched on the serving dish. He tasted it. "Hmm, this is good. I shall no doubt have to get used to this." The two Generals sat down to enjoy the remains of the President's dinner, while Ian Sharpe was dragged protesting from the New White House.

Jackson, ever alert to the changes of atmosphere, entered the room. "Generals, do you have any orders for me? A communiqué perhaps?"

"Yes, indeed. But first have the chef bring in another dish of this meatloaf. We have worked up an appetite."

General Browning smiled to see Sharpe's lackey rushing off to the kitchens. The man had no dignity. General Fraser put his feet up on one of the chairs and lit up a cigar. He didn't mind if he had to wait for his meatloaf, he had all the time in the world.

Chapter Six

That same evening on the late night news, the networks carried a brief announcement on behalf of the Junta.

Here, is a special announcement from The Joint Chiefs of Staff

Today, the terrorist group that wishes to be known as The American Eagles carried out another cowardly attack against the people of The Americas. At seven p.m., they mounted an unprovoked attack upon the headquarters of the Freedom Party in Houston, Texas. In the latest outrageous attack, over two hundred loyal members of the armed forces were killed, as well as an undisclosed number of members of the Executive of the Freedom Party.

The President was deeply shocked by this latest outrage, and he has been taken seriously ill. To protect the sovereignty of the nation, the Joint Chiefs of Staff have unanimously voted to intervene and until further notice, a Committee composed of members of the Armed Forces will oversee the government of the nation.

The Joint Chiefs of Staff also choose to extend to the belligerents an invitation for dialogue in order to resolve any points leading to their resorting to terrorist activities. In this regard, The Joint Chiefs of Staff is offering an amnesty for any member of the American Eagles that wishes to lay down their arms. This offer will expire in seven days from now.

This is the end of the communiqué.

Duane and James watched the programmed announcement with satisfaction. "James, what do you think about that? We need to be clear about our interpretation; otherwise we may have members of the resistance movement trying to obtain an amnesty. I'll tell you what I think: first, the JCS have lost patience with Ian Sharpe, this is a coup d'état, plain and simple. Sharpe is probably already in chains, and on his way to a prison cell; secondly, these are not men of honor, and the amnesty is bogus!"

"Yes, you are absolutely right on both counts. Anyone who falls for this will end up in an Army torture session, and they will have to spill everything that they know about the resistance movement; this is a very dangerous ploy, by the generals. We need to counter this with some hard hitting facts and reject the offer out of hand. But if there is one positive ray of hope, it is that they are conceding that they do not have the means to defeat us, or they would not have named us publicly, this is the first time that they have done so."

"Agreed. Contact the broadcast technicians and have them make up an announcement using Sharpe's voice denouncing everything that the Junta has just said. And let us also send the Armed Forces a present. Can we use a model plane again, or do you think that they might have wised up to that tactic?"

"I suggest that we use one of their drones. It can easily mingle with one of the flights patrolling every military base. I think Andrews Air Base would benefit from some remodeling, don't you think?" They both laughed.

One and half hours later, the American Eagles interrupted the regular programming to feature scenes showing the Army's handling of Robotoids, in particular the family that David and Nick had captured at Sioux Falls. Their automated replies clearly showed that they had been mentally impaired, the program also included the footage previously aired of the conversation by prison guards discussing the existence of Robotoids in the San Fernando Valley facility, and then the previously unpublicized footage of combat Robotoids storming a blockhouse situated in a valley near the Craters of the Moon National Monument. The film clearly showed men being cut down by automatic fire, but the rest of the force advanced regardless.

The commentary, using Ian Sharpe's voice described the process of transforming ordinary men, who had been detainees under the Emergency Powers Act, and now they were Robotoids. Finally, the documentary asked the viewer, *"Would you believe anything said by the Army Joint Chiefs of Staff? After all, these foul deeds were committed by them!"*

General Fraser was awakened from his sleep by his adjutant, who had recorded the entire media content by the American Eagles. Fraser was livid. "How did they obtain this information? Look, even though it was in low light conditions, they have captured the whole assault. It's as clear as daylight, and we have been exposed to the nation! Get a copy of this out to every member of the Joint Chiefs of Staff. You should tell them also that we will meet tomorrow to discuss our response to the broadcast."

The following morning, Duane awoke to find a bag on his side table. It was of the same type as the one that Jim Stewart had left before, only larger. A note was pinned to the bag. A data crystal was also on the table.

Good morning, Duane.

Please excuse my intrusion. I see that Ian Sharpe has been deposed, and the Junta has assumed control. Sharpe can still be of use, however. I popped in to see him in the maximum security wing at Leavenworth. He was quite surprised to receive a visitor, as you might expect. Anyway, with only a little telepathic persuasion, he made a statement confessing his involvement in the atrocities committed by the Freedom Party and the Junta. He was kind enough to agree to record his confession, and that is on the crystal. I have configured it to run on any device of your era.

In the bag, there are some more explosive devices, I'm sure that you will put them to good use. Don't allow any of your technicians try to open one though, it will be very messy, and I can assure you of that.

Farewell, for now!

J.S.

Duane reached for the comm. link and placed a safe call to James. "Good morning and how are you? Up and about I'm sure. I have had a night visit from our Jim, while I slept. He has left me a bag of goodies too. Also, he mentioned that he has been to visit Ian Sharpe who is being held in the maximum security wing at Fort Leavenworth. I have a data crystal holding his full confession. If you'd like to come over later, when you are free, we will watch it together."

"Wow! This just gets better and better, we will air this immediately. The drone has already been dispatched against Andrews Air base, and it joined a routine patrol along the perimeter. I expect that it will be dropping its payload right about...now! Well, you may be too far away, but I felt it, and I am five miles from Andrews. That should give them something to think about, eh?"

"Indeed. Come over when you can. Have you breakfasted already, I will have Bob prepare some for you when you arrive. When will that be, does thirty minutes sound about right?"

"Yes, traffic is still quite light where I am. I expect it's backed up on the Maryland side of the State boundary, especially when you get near to Andrews Air

Force Base. But I will be there soon. Have Bob prepare some eggs Benedict on toast. I feel like celebrating!"

Twenty minutes later James drove up to the security barrier of the cluster. He was known, and they waved him through.

Duane had already set the data crystal in the projector of the holo-television. "Don't worry, the set is isolated now. I had the techies block off the intrusion. If I want to receive outside broadcasts, I simply change the power supply to the central utility. I have also prepared a copy of this for you to take with you. Do you want to eat first or afterwards?"

"Oh, decisions, decisions. Let's eat first. Bob's eggs won't wait, but this will."

James enjoyed his breakfast while Duane merely sipped at his coffee. "James," he remarked wryly, "you will have to watch it, if you are to eat here so often, you will be gaining weight!" James smirked and grabbed another slice of toast which he spread with a generous amount of butter.

"OK, that's me done. Let's go see the confessions of a dictator!"

Ian Sharpe was very unhappy, and he had developed a nervous tick. Clearly he expected to be interrogated or injected with chemicals that would change his mind to mush. So he was sweating throughout the recording. Jim's voice could be clearly heard too, asking probing questions about his conduct as a member of the Freedom Party, and then during his brief tenure in the New White House. He didn't attempt evasion, since Jim clearly knew the answers before he asked questions and a couple of times Jim had to correct Sharpe when he made a self-serving answer or a factual error.

Sharpe confessed his whole sordid role in the Emergency Powers administration and named the senior military officers who had participated in the torture of detainees. General Fraser in particular came in for a lot of criticism. Sharpe attributed to Fraser the whole Robotoid military force. According to Sharpe, Fraser wanted to convert these detainees into fearless shock troops, but he was indifferent to the deaths of Robotoids in live ammunition exercises, they were expendable. The entire interview lasted thirty minutes, for a live broadcast they would remove some of it; ten minutes was all the air time that they could safely steal. The entire record would be kept for evidence in an indictment against the Junta and Ian Sharpe for crimes against humanity.

James commented, "It might be amusing if they ask him who interviewed him in the maximum wing of Leavenworth? Can you imagine him telling them that it was '*a man from the future who interviewed me, and he just appeared in my cell'?* They would transfer him to a padded cell for sure."

Duane laughed easily, "Now off you go to see David, my boy, let's get this out today. We will wait until they have reported on the destruction of Andrews Air Force Base. I imagine that the drone would have targeted the main administrative area only; it's a huge area if you count the hangars and the runways. Perhaps we need to drop some more of these balls tonight, you know, take out the rest of the base?"

"Yes, good idea. Give me three more bombs, which ought to be enough for now."

"Yes, and one more thing, Jim warned against tampering. They will explode if anyone tries to open one up. So, if the Junta gets hold of one, it may be fatal for them."

"I'll bear that in mind." James placed them carefully in a large envelope and secured them in his valise. "I'll be in touch later, and thanks for the breakfast." He added as he made for the door.

Duane placed a call to David Mackintosh. "Hi David, I think we are keeping you very busy these days. James is on his way over to drop off some very important footage of an interview with Ian Sharpe, yes, you heard me right. Make sure that the recording is date-stamped with yesterday's date. We shall be using part of the film for a broadcast now, but it will also be kept for a future war crimes tribunal, I believe that crimes against humanity under a state of martial law qualify it as such. We don't need to create a voice over on this film, the interviewer is unknown over here, and I doubt that the British government has any time to run a trace on him at the moment. All reports coming to me from Britain and the Euro Zone indicate that the revolution is well underway, and the whole rotten house of cards is about to fall. Did you catch the screening last night from the new Junta? I doubt that they will get any takers for their offer, after we transmit your reports. They were very powerful viewing. I was particularly impressed with the Robotoid soldiers in action. That was riveting, but disturbing at the same time."

"Yes, but it was scary for us doing the filming. We beat it out of there as soon as they breached the blockhouse. That was not a good place to get caught with cameras, God only knows what they might have done if they had detected our presence!"

"So, are you enjoying your work, David? Are you sure that you wouldn't prefer your cozy little anchor job at the All-American News Station?" Duane added playfully.

"Not on your life! That was a living death; I might have ended up like one of those Robotoids, like my fellow anchor, Julie. She was more than half way there, I reckon."

"Then I can take it that my thanks are not required? But we appreciate the work that you and Nick are doing. You make a great team, and we have broadcast some pretty powerful programs since you came on the team. Look, we should get together again soon. I know you are single and so are Nick and James, but that won't stop us from having a little social time. Let's get together on Saturday night. We can watch the football, and I'll have Bob make some pizza or something, nothing fancy, I'm worried about James' weight for one thing." He closed the line, still chuckling to himself.

However, that evening was no laughing matter for General Fraser. As head of the Junta, he was answerable to the rest of the Junta for the conduct of operations against the American Eagles. It was bad enough that they had hit Andrews Air Force Base that night, but then they had returned to deliver two more of the powerful bombs to take out the runways and the main hangars. And then to cap it all, they had suckered the Army Intelligence department into going to Washington Executive Airport, which is also known as Hyde Field. In the public car park area, a van was parked. They were told that inside they would get a sample of the new explosive. If they handled it correctly, they were assured it was perfectly safe. A squad of Army Intelligence operatives backed up by the bomb squad went to the scene. They never had time to investigate the brown package which was perched on the hood of the van; it exploded with devastating force, more powerful even than the other devices. Hyde Field was totally destroyed. The American Eagles had made him a laughing stock yet again.

Throughout the night, reports were coming in of similar explosions across the entire Americas; clearly the American Eagles had no shortage of supply of the new explosive material, and morale was beginning to suffer.

Two days later, Fraser was mortified to discover that the rebels had managed to turn his entire fleet of drones against him. Fifty thousand drones were now pummeling military bases across the Union. General Browning was of no help either, because he reported that the military were locked out of their own control and command satellite. This was serious, very serious, and he didn't know what to do.

The reports continued to come in, the drones had kept firing until they had exhausted their payloads, and then they had dived into the airfield buildings causing more damage; there were also reports of several drops of Cluster Bomb Units which contained nerve gas. The manpower losses were enormous. Some drones had been deployed along the highways and Interstates, and they had interdicted the relief columns. The army was a sitting duck in these situations, but the fixed wing aircraft on the airfields were unable to help much either, as the supposed protecting forces had destroyed fuel dumps and munitions, hangars and runways. The only forces able to render assistance were the naval fighters. They quickly decimated the drones that were operating within their range, but by then the damage had already been done. Fraser's staff estimated that they had suffered the loss of at least 30% of their own land-based aircraft, but thankfully most of the

American Eagles' commandeered drones and hovers had been destroyed by the end of the day.

Fraser reflected upon his first week in power. It had been a series of setbacks, to say the least. It was clear now that the American Eagles were making a bid to overthrow all unconstitutional government and bring the Junta down. What was worse, other groups, encouraged by the news reports of bombings were joining in. Daily now, the Special Marines were coming under sniper fire as they conducted their street patrols, and they were ambushed with IED's. The losses were steadily mounting from the IED attacks, and the terrorists were becoming more and more inventive. Yesterday, a children's stroller packed with high explosive and abandoned on the street in Chicago, had been remotely detonated. The marines had lost the entire patrol in that incident. There were reports of a mutiny in Texas, the military's morale was already down because of the loss of their payroll and the revelations in the media had convinced some brigades to switch sides. The mutineers were now holding the senior officers to ransom. They had demanded to be paid their wages and that the Army would release the detainees all over the Union. In Dallas they had released all of the slave labor that had been forced to work in the Elite's factories and they were threatening to release more workers.

Fraser was ill prepared for such confrontations, he was unfamiliar with negotiation techniques. But he was also disappointed that his offers to negotiate and grant amnesty to the rebels had failed to elicit a single response; the counter message which the American Eagles had released with an hour of his offers had been so visually powerful that no one had believed in the sincerity of the Armed Forces. No, this was a fight to the death, and it was beginning to look as if he would have to resort to hostage-taking or punitive measures upon cities where resistance was the strongest. But he was not sure that he could carry the Joint Chiefs of Staff with him in this, let alone the field commanders and the rank and file. Already morale was at an all time low, especially in the Air Force and those Army garrisons that had been decimated as they sat like sitting ducks for the attacks by the American Eagles' commandeered drones and use of high explosives. Yesterday, the Navy had come under attack too. The aircraft carrier Independence had been sunk offshore by a small plane that had attacked at sea level. The plane had hit the Independence amidships and on the waterline, with such devastating force that the mighty carrier was almost blown into two. Fraser had immediately ordered all ships to withdraw to a distance beyond the range of such planes. But that had not saved the ships already at anchor or those in the dry-docks along the East Coast before he issued the order. He again issued an appeal to the terrorists to cease hostilities, it read:

The following communiqué was issued this morning by the Military High Command:

The brave men and women of the Armed Forces of the Union of the Americas have laid down their lives in the defense of the freedoms of our great nation. They have pledged themselves to defend the nation from all threats foreign and domestic to that end. The High Command once again calls upon every patriot to assist them in eradicating our society of those would bring down our civilization and bring about anarchy. Citizens come forward and denounce the traitors! They hide among you as neighbors, using you as shields while they attack our peace-keepers in the streets. We will also reward any citizen that will do his patriotic duty by denouncing the terrorist factions.

Signed

General H. W. Fraser, on behalf of the Joint Chiefs of Staff

This is the end of the communiqué.

One hour later a single drone aircraft delivered a bomb by dive-bombing the West Point Military Academy. The destruction was total; the Joint Chiefs had their reply.

Chapter 7

The maximum security wing of the Army's penal institution at Fort Leavenworth is probably the most difficult place in the world to enter or leave. General Fraser accompanied by General Browning sat in amazement watching the holo-vid that featured Ian Sharpe's confession. The public broadcast ran for ten minutes and it was an indictment of the Freedom Party's Executive and the last two Heads of State, Ben Tyler and Arturo Sanchez. With the headquarters building having been destroyed, along with the entire Executive Committee, The Freedom Party had ceased to exist. Ian Sharpe's confession merely justified the coup by the military as being in the national interest, and Fraser's spin doctors were even now composing a documentary that they would use to emphasize the altruistic motives of the Joint Chiefs of Staff. The unsavory details about Robotoids being trained a shock troops would naturally be omitted from the documentary, but the Armed Forces paternal care of the nation would be the theme instead.

General Browning voiced the question that had been begging to be asked: "How on Earth did the American Eagles manage to penetrate the most secure penal facility in the world?"

"Well, you are the technical man, and a scientist. Have they invented a teleportation device?" Fraser replied.

"Look, teleportation is practically impossible, unless you have enormous computer power and an extremely sophisticated laboratory, which they don't! Experiments at MIT in the early part of the century only worked with inanimate objects over a short distance of a few hundred yards, no one has ever moved a live body the size of a human being. No, you can rule that out. We have to look first for the obvious, did you have all security tapes vetted, and were there any visitors to the wing. Are the guards trustworthy? These are the questions that need to be addressed, general." Browning fidgeted his hands nervously, despite his bold statement he always felt intimidated by the other man.

"I know my business, General Browning! And just for the record, yes, we did check all of these, and we also ran background checks on the entire staff of the Maximum wing. None of them have any relatives in detainee camps and they are all of impeccable loyalty. No, I am as baffled as you. I suggest that we do the most obvious thing of all, we go there and ask him!"

"OK, then we go to Leavenworth. Shall I make the arrangements?"

"It's already in hand; we leave as soon as you are ready."

Fort Leavenworth comprises three penal institutions. The Union of the Americas Penitentiary is located twenty five miles north of Kansas City. It was originally designed to function as a medium-security United States of America federal prison for male inmates in Kansas and it was operated by the Federal Bureau of Prisons, a division of the United States Department of Justice. After the Declaration of Emergency Powers, and the Act of Union, it underwent some radical changes. It still included a satellite prison camp for minimum-security male offenders, but the inmates were now being transferred to the regular detainee camps which contained mainly civilian inmates.

The Union of the Americas Disciplinary Barracks or UADB is the second of the penal institutions and it is a military prison. The third establishment within the Fort Leavenworth property and which opened on 5th October 2010, is the military's Mid-West Joint Regional Correctional Facility. Imprisonment at the MJRCF was limited to those enlisted prisoners who had received sentences less than five years. The three military establishments fall under the command of the Union of the Americas Army Corrections Command. Its commandant is Colonel Evan Dolman.

It was highly unusual to house a civilian prisoner such as Ian Sharpe, without his first appearing before a tribunal and receiving a sentence. The UADB is the military's only maximum-security facility. Normally all inmates would be male servicemen convicted at court-martial for violations of the Uniform Code of Military Justice. Confinement at the UADB was applied only to enlisted prisoners with sentences over five years, or commissioned officers. In certain special circumstances, however, a convicted civilian found guilty of national security offenses could be confined at UADB. But Ian Sharpe had not been even charged with offenses related to national security, let alone stood trial; it was all most irregular, and even criminal to confine him in this manner.

Colonel Evan Dolman was a stickler for procedure, and it irked him to be ordered to receive Ian Sharpe into the Maximum Security wing. It was not that he felt any compassion for the diminutive man, but apparently due process had been denied him, merely because it was more convenient to remove him from the public gaze. He had been assured that in due course Sharpe would stand trial before a military tribunal, but it would be a Special Tribunal with civilian judges on the panel. Colonel Dolman like everyone else had seen the broadcast made by the American Eagles and he was highly embarrassed. Only this morning, the military attaché at the New White House had called to inform him that a delegation from the Joint Chiefs of Staff would be visiting later today, he was to have Ian Sharpe ready to meet the generals.

However, Ian Sharpe was already receiving a visitor, unbeknown to Colonel Evan Dolman. Jim Stewart sat on the end of Sharpe's bed in the maximum security wing. He wore his customary white robe, but today his head was covered and he wore a pair of dark shades. His sudden appearance awakened Sharpe and he screamed with shock. "You again!" he exclaimed, "How do you do this? Have you come to torture me again?"

"The *how* is less important than the *why* at this moment. At this very moment several generals from the Junta are on their way to meet with you, and I have no doubt that you are going to face some robust questions. Are you happy to endure that, or would you like to take a little trip with me?"

"Look, you may be able to pop in and out of this facility with alacrity, but I am not like you." He pounded the wall to make his point. "In fact, you may be just a hallucination; I have been under a lot of stress lately. You aren't real, man!"

"Oh, ye of little faith!" Jim replied with a smile. "You just let me take care of the how, and the where. I want something from you, and in return I will take you somewhere safe. You can grow old fishing for salmon, or whatever it is that you Canadians do in the backwoods. Now do you want in or out? The choice is yours. You have about five minutes, at most, to decide."

At that very moment, the duty security officer was looking at an image on his screen from the internal surveillance camera that showed the interior of Ian Sharpe's cell. "Sergeant, did we give anyone access to visit the VIP cell?" The Sergeant looked blank and shook his head. "Come over here then," the officer ordered, "so who is that?" The camera showed an image of the rear of Jim's head. Jim Stewart was sitting talking to Ian Sharpe, but the sound was muted. Then he looked up and pointed an object at the surveillance camera. Immediately, the screen went blank. The officer hit the alarm buttons and the klaxon horns started wailing.

"Mr. President, you don't have even a minute to decide now. Choose now!''

It didn't take Ian Sharpe even a moment to decide, after all it was a choice between life and existence as a Robotoid for the rest of his natural life. "Then I choose to go out," he replied.

A moment later, he was sitting in a wilderness area. He recognised it as being similar to the type of wilderness where he had his cabin in the woods. He had grown up in an area very much like this, and few people knew these woods like he did. Certainly, there were no records in the Land Registry under his name, it was held in the name of a distant cousin. The cabin was fully stocked with survival gear. Here he could live out his days. "How did you know about this place, Mr....er?"

"My name is unimportant. I come from the future, so I know a lot from historical records. But you know a lot more than you gave me in your previous confession. I particularly want to know about the current leadership of the group which call themselves The Olympians or sometimes they go by the more ancient title of the Illuminati. You had recent dealings with them and they were your sponsors from the beginning; they have been your paymasters, as a matter of fact. You will tell me all that you know, and then I will leave you here to live in peace. But I will check the facts you supply me and if you have lied, well I might just drop you off in space somewhere. You wouldn't last long without air, I can assure you."

Sharpe swallowed hard and then he sat down on a rock and began to talk. Jim recorded everything.

The stratos jet touched down at Kansas City. There was a military airstrip adjacent to the Union of the Americas Disciplinary Barracks. It was normally used for the transfer of high risk inmates and occasionally by visiting VIP's. Colonel Dolman had come to meet them personally. As they descended from the jet, the wailing of the sirens filled the air; Colonel Dolman looked extremely nervous. "Colonel, why are the sirens sounding, is there an escape emergency?" General Browning asked.

"Yes, General, there has been an escape. Something bizarre has happened."

"What do you mean, 'something bizarre'" General Tavistock asked testily, "and who was the escapee?"

"Sir, the prisoner who escaped is the VIP, Ian Sharpe." They all looked at him disbelievingly. "Please come with me, gentlemen." Colonel Dolman showed them to a stretched ground-car limousine which he had arranged for their transportation. The European vehicle whisked the party silently to the UADB and parked at the entrance to the administration block.

"We have camera surveillance throughout the entire facility. It is monitored automatically by the system and manually by highly trained Military Corrections

Department staff. Every corridor and every cell is under continuous surveillance. In this Maximum Security Wing we also monitor sound and vision inside the confinement cells. We have recorded what transpired in the cell of the prisoner Ian Sharpe until just before the event. Please see the large display screen. As you will note, a man in a flowing white gown is sitting talking to the prisoner. Unfortunately, he is wearing shades and he has part of his face covered by the headdress. It appears to be some sort of Middle Eastern costume. Now watch! He has noted the camera and as soon as he points that small object at it the whole system just shut down, and all audio recordings were erased. We only have these few moments of visual imagery. Gentlemen, the cell block is in total lockdown at all times. No one goes in or out. Even meals are delivered through a sealed hatch into the prisoner's cell. The hatchway was not opened, yet the prisoner and his visitor have simply vanished. I don't know how to explain it. Did they walk through solid concrete with reinforcement walls?"

The delegation from the Joint Chiefs of Staff was also baffled. It would be easy to blame Colonel Dolman for negligence, but the evidence pointed to something supernatural; not in any way was it because of his negligence. General Fraser turned on his heel and walked out, and the delegation silently followed him. The ground car took them back to the jet.

Montague Meredith Morgan was the son of Matthew Morgan, the previous head of the Olympians until his untimely death by assassination with the whole of the Board of Directors of the Olympians and the President Designate of the Americas, Arturo Sanchez at the Presidential Hotel, Boston. He inherited the position of

Chairman of the Board of the Olympians as well as Chairman of The Elysian Fields Merchant Bank. After the destruction of the house in Boston by the American Eagles, his father had moved temporarily to a secure cottage in Nova Scotia. Montague discovered the existence of the second home only by accident, in a conversation with his father's chauffeur of all people. When he gained entry to the house, he discovered the full extent of his father's wealth and copious records of the affairs of the Olympians. Of course, as the eldest son, he had been groomed to succeed his father in all of the family business interests and he had graduated with honors from Harvard Business School, so he was well qualified. It was also a tradition among the Illuminati that the eldest son would inherit the mantle of the father, and he had been instructed in the ways of the secret order by his father and special instructors. The order was also known as The Ancient Order of the Illumined Wise Men, and from an early age he became an adept in the Luciferian rites of the Temple. He was now a Freemason of the thirty second degree and the most senior of the Masters of Masters of the Temple.

As part of his duties to the Order, he had traveled on behalf of his father to visit the European brethren and he had participated in their secret deliberations concerning the establishment of the New World Order. Behind the dictatorships that ruled over Britain, France and Germany, the Illuminati or Olympians manipulated the policies of the three governments. It was through the Olympians that the three dictators: Ian McGregor and his Progress party in Britain, Francois Bernard, his ally and Premier for Life of France and Herschel Schwartz, leader of the Euro Zone Parliament and the current leader of the inner circle comprising of Britain, France and Germany. All across the Euro Zone, the dictators had exploited detainees under the Emergency Powers Bills, by putting them to work in virtual slavery in their factories. This was no coincidence, but the policy of the Olympians. The Union of the Americas was the testing ground for the Olympians' policies, and Montague and his fellow conspirators had recently met to discuss the implementation of Robotoid technology throughout Euro Zone. The three dictators all stood to gain personally from having both Robotoid workers and Robotoid soldiers, because they held majority shares in the largest factories through the Euro Zone.

Unfortunately, in Euro Zone they were also facing resistance to their despotic rule, and as in The Americas, things were not going well. There was also mounting evidence that the resistance groups had formed an international alliance and were mounting joint operations against the military forces of the Axis Powers of the Euro Zone. Montague had been asked to share the American experience, but he had little encouragement for the Europeans since the assassination of the Board in Boston occurred during his absence in Europe. He had never been particularly close to his father, but the old man had provided well for him and his two brothers; and he saw only a golden future ahead for the Olympians. He shared his grand vision at the conference and the delegates were impressed by his enthusiasm for their holy work, even in the face of personal tragedy. He left promising to send technicians from the Americas to assist in the creation of a Robotoid workforce and shock troops. He was confident that eventually the Euro Zone guerrilla forces would commit the huge tactical error of a face to face confrontation, and they would be no match for a fearless army of Robotoids. These delegates reported back to their Temple lodges and a favorable report about Montague and his visionary leadership was passed to the supreme leader of the Order, who lived in Great Britain.

Montague Morgan didn't care for the cottage in Nova Scotia. He disdained the simple life style of the province and purchased for his personal use, a palatial property in The Hamptons. The previous owners had been forced to surrender their home after the bank foreclosed on the mortgage. It was no coincidence that Montague Morgan owned that bank. He insisted on immediate vacant possession and moved in within seven days.

He had reviewed the history of events prior to his father's death and he was amazed that Morgan Sr. had been so easily manipulated into taking an unwise course of action against a mercurial man such as Arturo Sanchez. Seen with the benefit of hindsight, it was clear that the two sides had been betrayed by the former Special Advisor to the President, Dr. Hans Strauss. Strauss had disappeared into thin air and he had not emerged anywhere in the Americas. Montague had dozens of men searching for him throughout the Union, but without success. He didn't believe that Strauss had acted alone; it was possible that he had switched his allegiance to the American Eagles, but for what reason he could not tell.

In his opinion, the American Eagles were the greatest danger to the Olympians' plans for a New World Order and he set about tracing them. They had been very clever at covering their tracks and none of his sources had any idea who the leader was. He had discovered that just prior to the destruction of the DHS headquarters in New Washington, a woman had tried to see the Director, David Roberts; she claimed to have knowledge of the leadership of the American Eagles. Montague instructed his agents to trace Elizabeth Fitzgerald, to see whether he might be able to glean some useful leads. Then he discovered that the computer records at the DHS had no record of her attendance at the designated time, and coincidentally, the bomb which landed on the DHS was dropped at exactly ten o'clock, the time of her appointment.

Montague smelled a rat. All searches into the history of Elizabeth Fitzgerald drew a blank. Someone had very efficiently expunged her name from every official database. Digging a little deeper, he discovered that the erasures had been sanctioned by the Federal Bureau of Investigation, but more than this he couldn't discover. This confirmed what he had suspected all along; in the FBI, there were secret members of the American Eagles. Why, even the security of the ill-fated conference in Boston had been botched by the FBI. The Director himself had explained to Montague that owing to 'insufficient resources' they were unable to supply more than a token presence around the Presidential Hotel, Boston. The Director also pointed out that Montague's father had insisted upon installing his own security inside the hotel, he had brought in a large number of crack Russian Special Forces commandoes. He refused to accept Montague's accusation of incompetence by his agents, and he insisted that it was not the job of the FBI to act as a private security force for a group of bankers. Montague reluctantly had to accept the Director's defense, but he still wondered whether the FBI had been infiltrated. He made a note of the Special Agent in charge of the hotel security team; it was Special Agent James Duncan.

James was called in to see the Director. "James, someone is sniffing around asking a lot of questions about your handling of the Presidential Hotel affair. It was the son of one of the bankers. His name is Montague Morgan. Just watch your back, James; this man is smart, probably wiser than his father, Matthew Morgan. Since he inherited the bank, I'm guessing that he has also taken over the leadership of the Olympians. Duane ought to be aware of this. Officially, I can do nothing, without tipping my hand, but I'll keep you informed of any developments. Just be careful!"

When James left the Director's office, he called Duane. He was out, but Bob said that he would pass on the message as soon as possible.

Chapter 8

Duane had been called to a meeting with the Joint Chiefs of Staff at the New White House. As he entered the Reception area inside the entrance hall, marines guards snapped off crisp salutes and a marine in a uniform that looked as if it had just been pressed, escorted him to the Presidential Briefing Room. Many of the furnishings had been salvaged from the White House and, as he walked the corridors of the new building, that link with the past was reinforced by the portraits of past presidents that looked down from the walls. What would they think of today's occupants, Duane wondered? The old stately White House had long since been demolished but its traditions lived on.

He had not been briefed before the meeting, so he knew nothing about the agenda. So he was surprised to see the leaders of The Senate and Congress in attendance also, but they were as much in the dark as him. Since political parties had long since ceased to have any role, their presence was mostly symbolic. Duane supposed that General Fraser wished to have his position ratified by the people's representatives, and he didn't expect anything remarkable to emerge from the meeting. He was wrong.

General Fraser accompanied by the whole group of the Joint Chiefs, opened the meeting, after greeting them warmly. "Gentlemen, we appreciate your acceptance of our invitation to attend this morning. I believe that it will serve no purpose if I speak obtusely, therefore I will be direct and get straight to the point. In the past, we have been at cross-purposes, but in the current climate we believe that there is an opportunity to rebuild the nation. The Freedom Party is gone. In spite of what the first communiqué said, the whole of the decision-making Executive Committee of the Freedom Party perished in that bombing. I don't know if the American Eagles knew that there was a secret meeting of the Executive scheduled for that evening, probably not, but if not, then it was amazing luck! The need for the Freedom Party has gone also; whoever would try to restore it is doomed to fail. We don't want it, anyway; this great country, The Union of the Americas was founded in a time of democracy, the Declaration of Emergency Powers followed later and it was meant to be a temporary solution to deal with a breakdown of law and order, schism, and feudalism that had emerged all across the Union since the big Ones of 2050. You know this of course, I am merely stating the obvious, to go to my main point.

This nation has seen some terrible times under the Freedom Party; its leaders forced us to walk where we ought not to have trodden. Most of us grew up knowing nothing except Martial Law. In truth, the Armed Forces also share some portion of the blame, because we allowed ourselves to be so manipulated. The agenda that we followed was not set by Congress, the Senate or the Judiciary; it was, we are sure now, a programme which was set in place by an international body that had successfully manipulated generations of Presidents along a course they would not have chosen had they been able to see where we stand today."

General Fraser paused momentarily to allow the significance of his words to sink in, and then he continued. "I have to tell you that the traitor, Ian Sharpe, who we placed into protective custody pending a trial for war crimes, has escaped from the maximum wing at Fort Leavenworth. I know that this sounds fantastic, but it is true. We don't know how he escaped, or the identity of his accomplice. But what I have to tell you now makes all of that irrelevant."

General Fraser paused again, unsure how to proceed. He looked to his fellow officers and sought their backing. They nodded and he continued. "Gentlemen, the time has come for nation building. We believe that this can only be done through national reconciliation and also by the cessation of the State of Emergency."

Duane and the two legislative representatives were shaken by this, Senator McDonald actually gasped, but it was the representative of the Congress, Congressman Morales that spoke first. "Let me be clear. You intend to promulgate a revocation of the Emergency Powers Act and you want to establish a National Reconciliation Tribunal? If this is to be so, then it will take time to form political parties. Democracy functions best when there is a constitutional opposition, at least two parties are needed for that. Or do you have in mind a different model, Generals?"

General Abrams spoke for the Generals now, "You know democracy with the two-party system didn't work perfectly, it was cumbersome and tended to be focused on personalities rather than issues. Some of us rather favor establishing a pyramidal system: a grassroots committee for local affairs, leading up to a President supported by a committee of senior politicians, Senators if you will. In this model, the House of Representative will be based in each State, not in New Washington. We believe that the old system was very wasteful of taxpayers' money. But we are willing to put the matter out for consultation. In the issue of a National Reconciliation Tribunal, we need to create a working group to determine how it will operate and what will be the limits of its powers."

Duane decided that he ought to contribute also, "Gentlemen, I am merely a jurist. I know nothing of politics, but the Judiciary must exist as it was originally envisioned by the Founding Fathers: it has to be independent of the Executive and free to interpret the existing laws or to reject unconstitutional laws. In my opinion, justice has to be seen to be done. We can learn some lessons of history. In some countries they attempted to establish something similar to your proposed National Reconciliation Tribunal, and the results have been mixed, I think it is fair to say. How do you say to a man that has seen his father converted into a Robotoid, 'Oh, it's alright. Just forgive the doctors who did this, it's for the national good.' It seems to me that the man will feel that the law has failed him. But, if on the other hand, there is found a therapy that may rehabilitate his father, then the degree of injury is lessened. There may be many factors to bear in mind before we can draw up guidelines for the Tribunal. Certainly, there are models of War Crimes Tribunals that worked well; in such tribunals it was the leader who issued the order for genocide, for example, who was judged most severely. So the guidelines will require careful consideration."

Then Senator McDonald raised the issue of the Olympians, though he didn't use that title. "General Fraser, you mentioned in your opening remarks, and I am quoting you, 'an international body that successfully manipulated generations of Presidents'. Do you have evidence of the existence of such a group? Indeed, may I comment that, if indeed such a group does exist, then they would be very powerful and constitute a continuing threat to the security of our nation, and perhaps other nations as well? They may well hinder your efforts to turn the clock back."

"In answer to your questions, may I say that we were prompted to consider this course of reform mainly as a result of the testimony of Ian Sharpe? We received yesterday, a crystal containing a full disclosure by him concerning his activities before and during his tenure as President. Part of this revelation was aired in the broadcast made by The American Eagles, and we believe it to be genuine and an original recording. In the portion of the revelation that has not been broadcast, he makes numerous references to the activities of a clandestine group. He says that they are known by many names, but they wish to be called 'The Olympians' or 'The Elite'. He has named prominent persons who have been promoting the interests of the Olympians. He also lists the organisations known to him which act as legitimate fronts for their activities, channeling illicit funds into the markets by money laundering and creating fake securities for gold deposits. But in the same delivery, we also received a second testimony. The author of this confession is also known to you: Dr. Hans Strauss, the Special Advisor to a succession of Presidents from McHenry down to Tyler. Strauss disappeared, but we believe that he was snatched by the American Eagles, although he appears to be speaking without coercion. His confession confirms that of Ian Sharpe, but his brilliant mind has retained masses of information about The Olympians. He confesses that he was in the Olympians' employ from his twenties, or about fifty years. They trained him and groomed him for the advisory position that he finally obtained. He gave no indication as to his whereabouts, but he stated that he had suffered a mild stroke during his captivity, which he half-believed was in Brazil. Now putting these independent testimonies together, to our minds, it leaves no doubt that The Olympians do exist and that they are a threat to us all.

We have yet to agree on a suitable strategy for the elimination of this group."

General Abrams added, "And what about the American Eagles? Their activities would undermine us still further, and instead of going after the criminal financiers, we could be wasting our time chasing a will o' the wisp! Who will prevent them from continuing to blow up our camps and mounting attacks to destroy our logistical support?"

"Well," said Duane, "My guess is that they will cease operations when they see that you are making a sincere effort at reform, not any sooner or later, if they are reasonable men. Since we know very little about them, shouldn't we assume that they are in fact reasonable men?"

The group agreed that this was a reasonable assumption, given that their actions to date had targeted those elements of society that were acting as oppressors, and they had made no demands for power.

"Now, concerning this international conspiracy," Senator McDonald asked, "what do we really know of its roots, other than the testimony given to the Joint Chiefs by Hans Strauss and Ian Sharpe?"

Duane replied, "Personally, I have little knowledge of them, except that some researchers have linked many of the American Presidents and members of the Supreme Court to the Illuminati, who I believe are the same people as the Olympians. If this be true, then I fear that this conspiracy goes to the very core of our society; you might say that it is so deeply entrenched that it is systemic!"

"Well, Your Honor, I hope that you are not a member of this cult?" General Abrams exclaimed in alarm.

"No, General, I most certainly am not! But if you will accept that, I would gladly have one of my staff do further research. We need to identify the ringleaders at least, before we can unite against this enemy. I am sure that you military men can agree with that precept?"

"Indeed we can. It is partly the reason that we called you all to this informal discussion. I propose that we shall declare a unilateral ceasefire, as a preparation to rescinding of the Emergency Powers and Martial Law. If the American Eagles and other groups abide by the ceasefire, then we will proceed to other measures which will ensure an orderly return to normal life, such as replacing the marines patrolling the streets with police patrols, ceasing random searches of individuals and houses. Putting an end to the rationing of food and other such imposed restrictions. But if we do not get reciprocity, we shall be forced to return to the repressive measures initiated by President Ben Tyler in the Declaration of Emergency Powers in 2052."

"And what about the detainees? Will they also be freed, General Fraser?" McDonald asked.

Fraser looked uncomfortable answering this question. Perhaps the Joint Chiefs had differences on some issues. He spoke hastily, anxious it seemed to terminate the meeting. "That will be first of all dependent on a cessation of hostilities; then we have to look at the reason for the arrest and take appropriate action. Illegal immigrants can be deported immediately. Hostiles who were caught with weapons, will await the National Reconciliation Tribunal's instructions; for those detainees requiring remedial medical care, it may take longer. If any of you gentlemen are aware of a therapy that may assist in the recovery of a group of patients, we would welcome your assistance.

And now, I think we may adjourn this meeting. I will make the announcement tonight and we shall see what the response will be from the Union's citizenry. Good day, Gentlemen." They all shook hands and went their separate ways.

Bob gave Duane the message as soon as he entered the house, so Duane immediately placed an enciphered call to James, and David, as a conference call.

"Gentlemen, I have some great news to share with you. Could you both drop whatever you are doing and come to my home?" He declined to be drawn any further and went up to his dressing room to change. To his great surprise he found Jim Stewart sitting waiting for him. By his side, on the night stand there lay another crystal.

"Well, this is a nice surprise, Jim. I would invite you down for lunch but since you say that you are all energy now, all I can offer you is the wall socket to charge you up!" Jim laughed good-naturedly.

"Well, as they say, 'the thought was there anyway.' I suppose that you have had your meeting with the Generals this morning? It was quite a turnaround for them. But vigilance must be maintained, Duane. Fraser still has dreams of the Robotoid army. But what he doesn't know, and what you have hoped for, I am going to tell you now."

"Oh, now you have intrigued me, do tell me Jim?"

"Well, the good news is that David Miller and the Angel Network in Britain have managed to synthesize the protein which was produced as 'The Kyoto Protocol'. Let's refer to it by its initials, it is so less cumbersome. Well, this protein, KP, operates in the brain, extending the pathways, which is what has led to the amazing expansion of intelligence in the recipient. Now when you get your supply, you will manufacture your own powder which can be distributed by dilution in the water supply. What you will happily discover is that the protein has another unpredicted property. Part of its action in the brain is that of restoring damaged electrical pathways. You have hoped for a therapy to cure the Robotoids. KP is the answer! David Miller will contact you soon with full information so that you can begin your program of water treatment. This is going to make an important change to your society. Can you imagine how a society that is telepathic will behave? Consider how it will impact the legal system. Shall a man's broadcasted thoughts about a crime that he stands accused of be tantamount to a confession? How will a jury determine guilt, will the burden of proof rest upon testimony of two or more witnesses; will physical evidence have the same weight as a telepathic examination? These are all matters to be defined. I fear that lawyers are going to be busier than ever but it will be an exciting time for society."

"Jim, I have no doubt that you are right, especially since you are speaking with the benefit of hindsight. And speaking of exciting times, did you happen to pop into Leavenworth yesterday and pop out with Ian Sharpe in tow?"

Jim answered with a twinkle in his eye, "Well we did a trade. On that crystal is the information that will help you in your quest for the Olympians, otherwise known as the Illuminati. But that is all for now, I gotta go!" Then he vanished.

"There you go again, Jim. Very annoying!" In the background, he seemed to hear an echoing laugh. He quickly changed into something more comfortable and picking up the crystal, he went downstairs to find James Duncan and David Mackintosh waiting for him. Bob was serving chilled beer in tall glasses. "I'll have a Coors, please Bob."

124

By common agreement, they opted for sandwiches and more chilled beers, so that Duane could go to the issues that had come up. "Guys, I have called you here so urgently because something happened today which may well be the turning point in our struggle. Yesterday, I sent the Joint Chiefs of Staff copies of the confessions of Hans Strauss and Ian Sharpe. These were the unexpurgated versions. In a sense, it was an appeal to their better natures, it was my hope that they had thought that they were on the side of the righteous, but after viewing the confessions, they would be without excuse. It turned out that I was right. Possibly, General Fraser dissents where the Robotoid soldiers are concerned; but a majority of the Junta was shocked to realize that they had been so misled for the past five decades. So, the majority decision was to offer to revoke the Declaration of Emergency Powers, and then set up a tribunal for National Reconciliation. The details have yet to be worked out, and we are supposed to achieve a consensus with the political leaders by consultation. All the Joint Chiefs ask as a precondition to a return to barracks is that we also lay down our arms. They have pledged to deport illegal aliens from detention, release detainees and investigate ways to restore Robotoids if it is possible. So, in effect they are suing for peace with some minor preconditions! Isn't that wonderful? Now, something happened yesterday which bowled them over. Ian Sharpe escaped from the Maximum Security Wing at Leavenworth. It was done right in front of a camera, and he had an accomplice. Neither Sharpe nor his accomplice was observed to leave: the gates were all locked, and the walls and roof were undisturbed, they had simply vanished. What do you make of the story so far, David?"

"It's weird and wonderful! Maybe you put something stronger in the beers? Do you think that

Sharpe's vanishing trick contributed to their decision to seek peace?"

"Personally, I don't. I think that it was as they told us, because of the two confessions. But Fraser for one must be quaking in his boots, because Sharpe's confession is an indictment on his part in the development of the Robotoids, particularly for military uses. But let me tell you now, James and I know the identity of the accomplice, and also how he was able to come in and out of a locked cell undetected. No, I'll stop teasing you and tell you what I know. In fact, just minutes after your arrival, while I was getting changed, the same person entered my dressing room. We had another conversation, and he told me some good news, and before he left he gave me this crystal. This crystal contains the last conversation that our mystery man had with Ian Sharpe. We will watch it in a moment.

James, will you show David the rock? This rock was given to me by the visitor. I have had the minerals in this rock analysed by experts. They were very excited when they examined it, but I did not disclose its origin. Believe me when I say that it is extraterrestrial, those minerals and elements do not appear anywhere on earth. Now James, please show David one of the small balls in the bag which is on the table over there. David be very careful, don't squeeze the ball. If you do, you will arm it. It is ultra high explosive. It may be of earthly origin, but not in this time. It is from the future, David, about seven thousand years in our future! My visitor brought it as proof of what he is. I won't tell you his name, because his namesake-his original self-is alive today, and lives in England. You may meet him one day, and James, he told me that you certainly will. But his namesake doesn't need to know about this episode. He also provided the explosives to help us turn the tide in our struggle, and I think we can all agree that happened because of this small weapon. Please return it to its place now, James, it makes me nervous".

"OK," David replied, "then this man has done all of this to help us. He asks nothing in return also. Who is he, the Caped Crusader?" They all smiled at the historical reference.

"I am sure that he is on the side of the righteous, he's not an angel, by the way, but he claims to be on passing acquaintance terms with some. Now shall we watch the true life confessions of Ian Sharpe?" James switched on the power to the holo-screen on and placed the crystal in the projector mechanism.

A few moments later, Ian Sharpe's holographic image stood before them. He was still dressed in the Day-Glo Orange suit of the maximum security prisoner, but behind him, the view was of beautiful woods with mountain peaks in the distance. Birds sang nearby, and it was a naturally beautiful and tranquil location. The interviewer's voice introduced Ian Sharpe, but apologized that his location had to be kept confidential, under the terms of their agreement.

Sharpe mostly spoke freely, occasionally he was steered in a general direction, but he spoke without coercion. He described his youth as the only son of a poor family. He obtained a scholarship to University and graduated with honors at the top of his classes with masters' degrees in commercial law and finance. After graduation, he joined a prominent investment bank, J.P. Morgan, and he rose quickly under the personal interest of the Chairman. He realized that his rapid promotion was necessary because the firm wished him to enter politics and so represent their interests. He soon discovered that the path to power and riches would be found by joining the Freemasons and showing himself to be a seeker of light. He advanced quickly through the lower degrees of the Order. In 2040, his freemasonry sponsors enrolled him in a high-achiever's finishing school, in Switzerland, where he underwent intensive indoctrination in Luciferian dogma and he was instructed in Olympian strategy. He was encouraged to seek "more light" and he progressed through to the highest degrees of the Illuminati Order, which is known as Freemasonry. By the time that he had reached the thirtieth degree, he was thoroughly accepted in the ranks of the secret society, and consequently even more money and power flowed toward him. He was recognized as someone who was going straight to the top by the express elevator. Beautiful women were available always at his beck and call, and he used drugs and alcohol freely. The Olympians took over the grooming process, and by 2050, he had become the youngest Prime Minister of Canada on record in the twenty first century.

Then came the Big Ones, and society collapsed all across the Americas. But as he recalled, the higher echelons of the Olympians were actually pleased at the catastrophes because they saw it as a golden opportunity to accelerate their plans. Ben Tyler was related to many past presidents of the USA, though distantly, and he too was now under the patronage of the Olympians. They became friends and co-workers in the cause of the Olympians.

In 2052, by a sovereign act of Union, Canada joined with the United States of America and Mexico to form The Union of the Americas. Shortly thereafter, Ben Tyler made the famous Declaration of Emergency Powers and the Olympians' pace moved into high gear. Then Ian Sharpe began to name families and organisations in the Union, as well as abroad, who were partners in this massive conspiracy. The movement was political, social, and it was rooted in ancient religious rites that bound its members together. In the lower ranks of the Order, the members were unaware that they were participating in a secret society bound by ancient rites that had their roots in the Luciferian religion; they only reaped the privileges that were granted to them in recognition of their loyal service.

Secrecy pervaded the order, but the highest degrees of the Freemasonry order were actually secret levels of Luciferian illumination with links to other occult groups. The Luciferian members despised the lower degree membership, whom they referred to between themselves a little better than cattle. Such Luciferian secrets were shared only with those who attained to the degrees from thirty to thirty three. The Order's leadership was passed on in generational succession unless someone created a breach by betraying the secrets of the Order. Sharpe also explained that following the assassination of the previous leadership, the Chairmanship of the Olympians Board had devolved upon the eldest son of Matthew Morgan, whose name is Montague Meredith Morgan. The family had full ownership of a private merchant bank, named The Elysian Fields Merchant Bank and its head offices were in Boston. He then went on to list all the new members of the Board of The Olympians.

His interviewer then asked what would be the Olympians' reaction to his disclosure of such information and if they suffered a military defeat of the Armed Forces by The American Eagles. Sharpe laughed at him derisively, "You cannot defeat them, and they control everything now. The governments are theirs, the banks belong to them, and their power and authority reach the highest levels in The Americas and in the Euro Zone too. Who do you think is pulling the strings of the dictators? They are all Illuminati anyway, but the ancient nobility of Europe still controls everything from the highest levels. All US Presidents have been hand-picked by the Olympians for the past two hundred years and it is the same story in Europe. Ian McGregor killed off the British Royalty, that was a mistake, but he kept old King Charles IV alive, as an afterthought. But after the loss of his entire family, old 'C4', couldn't be trusted to run the Illuminati any longer, so others took it over."

"And what is the objective of the Illuminati, or the Olympians, as they like to be called?"

"To establish a New World Order of course! We will hand it over to Our Lord Lucifer, and he will rule the Earth in peace and prosperity forever".

"Clearly you believe that to be true. But you made a religious statement, are you then a religious society?"

"Essentially, yes, only through the unity of the ancient and true religion could we have survived through the hundreds of years since we were founded. The lowest ranks don't know that of course, but when the New World Order arrives, they will have to conform to our highest rites, or they will be sacrificed like all unbelievers".

"Then, for whom is the promise of the golden age of peace and prosperity?"

"I think that by now it must be obvious to you! Haven't you been paying attention? We, the faithful elite, will enjoy the fruit of the kingdom of Lucifer. The masses will serve us, you know as Robotoids. They will not realize that they have lost their humanity. We will breed as many of them as we need, to maintain the system, but we will cull the useless eaters of Asia and India, to preserve the world's resources, you understand".

"One last question, Ian Sharpe? If I spare you and let you live, will you return to politics or will you live out your life here in exile?"

"Oh now you speak of judgment upon me. I thought that we had a deal? You tricked me by asking me if I wanted in or out! I had no idea that you were taking me to permanent exile in this wilderness! The price of betrayal of the secrets of our Holy Order is death. It would be a long and painful death also. I cannot ever return now. But I still believe that Lord Lucifer will reinstate me, once I explain how you tricked me".

"Mr. Sharpe, if you really believe those last statements, then you are an absolute fool! Lucifer is not the kind, merciful angel of light that you believe him to be. Far be it for me to wish evil upon anyone, but you deserve whatever comes your way. You will find no friends here on this planet, only wild animals that will hunt you down. See that cabin over there? That will be your refuge or your prison during the long months of winter. In spite of your arrogance toward the poor and the oppressed on Earth, I have shown you a degree of mercy that you do not deserve. Also, I have provided some basic foods to get you started, and seed to plant your first corn crop, there is a well with clean water nearby. You will find simple weapons inside the cabin. I suggest you become adept at using them. Farewell!"

"Wait, you said, 'on this planet', am I not in Canada or even on Earth, then?"

"Oh, no! We shall cleanse the Earth of all such as you. Do you think your Lord Lucifer will be able to find you here?" Jim closed his interview with a mocking laugh and the screen went blank.

Chapter 9

"OK, let us begin. We can see from the recording that Ian Sharpe is unrepentant, and probably he will not change. But at least he is in a place where he can't infect others with his strange notions. Now, let us examine the data that he volunteered. One name stood out, that of Montague Morgan, who he identified as the leader of the cult here in the Americas. He should be our primary target, I suppose. James, what do you know of him?

"Nothing bad actually, except that he went to see the Director asking about me. It seems that he blames me for the poor security at the Presidential Hotel, when his father was assassinated, along with the whole of the Olympians' Board. In a way he was right, but Morgan's security chief must bear the ultimate responsibility, because Morgan had installed his own security within the hotel: crack Russian troops all of them, heavily armed and well experienced in that type of security operation. I think that Sanchez's Mexicans just overwhelmed them with a surprise attack, and Sanchez himself had whet the blade of his sabre on the Russians before he burst into the meeting hall. No, Montague is paranoid, but I wouldn't write him off. He's probably scheming right now to have me bumped off! I suggest that we put him under observation, and put a shield over me too."

"Yes, we will. Have Rick Blade depute two guys to watch him. I'd recommend audio as well as video surveillance. Now, David, the reason that I invited you to this conference was to fill in some of the blanks in your knowledge of the big picture. The American Eagles does not stand alone, in the Union; other groups who wish to remain independent are also fighting alongside us, particularly in Mexico and in the western parts of Canada. But I have regular conferences with their leaders and we have one mind on the current issues. I have apprised them of the Military's offer of a cease fire and they have all agreed that they will cease hostile actions just as soon as the offer becomes public knowledge. I appreciate that, because otherwise it would be clear that I have been playing a double game. So, the next target is the group headed by Morgan, the Olympians, also known as The Illuminati. This cult is drawn from the highest echelons of the Freemasons; as we just heard, in the lower degrees of the Order, the members have no idea of the true nature of this secret society. Most recruits to the lowest ranks are approached by friends who convince them that Freemasonry is a guaranteed path to commercial or social success, but it is much more than secret handshakes and charitable works! I shall give you an introduction to an ex-freemason, of the thirty second degree; that means he risked his life to leave them. We have an umbrella of protection about him, but he is unaware of that. I'd prefer to keep it that way. His name is Arnold Noble. Arnold will explain all about the secret rituals and the plans of the society. Then we will start publicizing them, which is your area of expertise. My reason for doing this is mainly that I want to get them off balance. But it will also reassure the Joint Chiefs that they acted for the right reasons. Maybe we won't be able to manipulate the son as we did the father, but Montague Morgan may well be tempted to do something rash, and then we will have him!"

David asked, "You mentioned the big picture. What did you have in mind?"

"Yes, I drifted away from my theme. Not only are we allied with the other national groups, but for several years we have been in close contact with many international resistance groups, such as the Angels Network in the United Kingdom. The Angels are led by Field Marshall David Miller and I speak often with him. Now, we recently organized a video conference that included all of the principal groups. I chaired that conference, as it happens. The day is fast approaching that we shall make a decisive strike that will radically transform the world. I'm not just talking about toppling the dictators, I saying that there will be societal change.

David, what I am about to tell you is a secret that very few know of in our organization, in fact it will be the three of us only. There has been an exciting discovery made by an American doctor and her Japanese husband. Three years ago, he died in Kyoto, murdered by agents of the East Asian Republic. He and his wife had discovered a new protein; they named it after the place of its discovery, Kyoto. The couple developed a therapy that they dubbed The Kyoto Protocol or KP for short. The governments of the world are seeking the three young children who carry this protein in their bodies. David, we believe that KP is the wonderful, yet simple, answer to the world's current problems, but I won't divulge more than you need to know yet. KP has been synthesized and we plan to use it widely very soon. Jim Stewart, of the future, has just told me that one of the unpredicted benefits of KP is that it regenerates old pathways in the brain. He assured me that it will restore the Robotoids!"

"Wow! That would be the greatest blessing ever. If they also retain no knowledge of their actions whilst in a Robotoid condition, then they will suffer minimal trauma. Duane, this is just the best. I have been feeling so sad, ever since Nick and I saw those Robotoid soldiers storming that blockhouse, and being cut down by the defenders in the process. Well, it has kept both of us awake at nights, I can tell you!"

"Yes, it's good news, but just for a short while you can't share this with Nick. There's too much riding on this knowledge, and we are still unsure about General Fraser's commitment to peace. Every General's dream is having toy soldiers that they can just push into battle regardless of the cost, so he may try to withhold some Robotoids for his own purposes, but our KP strategy will defeat that. Here is the address of Arnold Nobel. I have told him to expect you. He is willing to record his conversation, and he will cooperate fully. Arnold is his new identity, and you don't need to know his old name. We suspect that the Illuminati are searching for him, so we are shielding him to the best of our abilities. I am sure that only part of what he tells you would be usable in a ten minute broadcast, but you will know best what would have the most impact for the viewing audience."

James was meanwhile calling Major Rick Blade. "Hi, Rick, it's me again. Have a look at the file which I'm sending you now. This man is Montague Morgan, son of Matthew Morgan who met with a tragic accident in Boston, if you recall. Yes, I thought that you might. Look, we believe that Morgan junior is a threat. He has already been to see my Director, and he smells a rat over the hotel bombing and our poor security outside. We believe that he may be targeting me. I need a shield. Also you need to assign two good operatives right away to concentrate upon Morgan. Have audio as well as visual surveillance, video if you can get it. We want to know just what he is cooking up. We plan to take him down eventually, so this is useful reconnaissance work. OK, Buddy, I am at Duane's now and I will be leaving in thirty minutes, does that give you enough time? If you pick up a tail on me, take them out. If they are good, there may be more operatives tailing me, so make sure. This may require a week's stakeout. OK, thanks. Let me know when you pick up a tail. I will have Nick do a sweep of my apartment for bugs and we will check my vehicle regularly for IED's and tracking devices."

David left to keep his appointment with Arnold Nobel. James returned to join Duane in the living room. "Duane, I have a question, was it wise to give so much information to David? I mean, that knowledge is priceless, and if it fell into the wrong hands…"

Duane interrupted him, "Yes, I can understand your concerns, but I didn't explain everything about KP and besides, I really only added a little to what Dr. John Phillips had told him earlier at Sioux Falls. Dr. John is an astute judge of character and I trust his judgement. And let us not forget that David and Nick put their lives on the line when they spied on the military and the DHS detainee camps. No, David and Nick are alright. But have him watched anyway, if only for his own protection."

"Leave that to me. I'm sorry to question your judgement, Duane, it just that, well we have come so far and with the end in sight, we don't want any problems coming up at this stage."

"James, don't worry about that. I am a man like you, and I could make a mistake and misjudge someone. But if it's any consolation, KP in its synthetic form is expected at any time within the next week. The courier will leave London Central soon, and David Miller will send me a signal with a code word. Then we shall begin the second phase of our struggle. Our chemists are standing by to receive details of the process and we will start production right away. We will have labs all over the Union producing the magic powder by the ton!"

"Really? Oh, you've made my day, Boss. So we have to tie up a few loose ends meanwhile, like our slippery Olympians and the Illuminati. Rick's men will be moving into position immediately, because as it happens, he has some people available along the East Coast. He did some routine checks on Montague Morgan a few days ago and we found out that Morgan has recently registered a large property in The Hamptons. We're guessing that he won't be returning to live in the Boston house that his father lived in prior to our attack upon it. We don't know where he has lived in the meanwhile, but he may lead us to that bolt hole too. So, I'd better be on my way. I will call in occasionally to keep you informed, and so that you know that I'm still alive!"

"Yes, do that, especially the bit about staying alive, my boy!"

Montague Morgan was not thinking about James or anyone else at that minute, he was in his newly completed Temple or Shrine, as he liked to call it. The old house in The Hamptons had a spacious basement and he had employed the best Masonic artisans to fit it out to his specific requirements. Since his election to the 32nd degree of the Freemasons, his pressing desire had been to enter the 33rd level, and now his life's dream was coming to pass. As the youngest leader of the Illuminati in recent history, his star was on the rise, and he had it on good authority that Herbert Kell himself had agreed to come to solemnize the Temple and at the same time he would take his vows for the 33rd degree. Montague had learned that only 5% of the 32nd degree Masters ever made it into the Illuminati, but he had shown the utmost zeal for the Order and it had been noted by the highest echelons. It was also the tradition that the Master of Masters would pass down his apron to his eldest son, and Montague had worked toward that end since his youth. In spite of his age, he was feared by all of his peers and he was given deference by all who perceived that here was a rising star of the Order.

Herbert Kell was also feared above all members of the higher orders, and with good reason; he was rumoured to be one of the "Seven", but he was definitely one of "The Nine Unknown Men". The tales about his awesome gifts were legendary, it was even said that he had the power to levitate and travel immense distances. Montague didn't believe all of this, but he knew for a fact that Kell had once killed a man just with a look. This knowledge made him fearful and worthy of his respect. Therefore, Montague was determined that everything in his initiation would go perfectly. He reflected upon the vows made in his 32nd initiation ceremony. His father had been so proud of him on that day, but Montague was sorry that the old man had not lived to see the day that his eldest son attained to such an exalted degree.

The voice of the Grand Master still rang in his ears, *"Novitiate In the 32nd degree, now you desire to become Priest and King. You shall be a partaker from this time forth in the Royal Secret. You shall indeed be a Priest and King of Ahura-Mazda. Offer now your incense to Serpenta Mainyu, the divine wisdom, and sacrifice thou with an offering of incense to the God in whom thou doest put thy trust."*

Montague had thrown his incense upon the eternal flame, which burned on the altar, and his incense rose before his God, Lucifer. He had then kneeled and prayed that he would be given more light. The room had at first become darkened as the spirits accepted his offering, and Montague had felt within him a new stirring as the fresh anointing settled upon him, and a glow from the altar fell upon his bowed head.

Again the Grand Master had bid him to offer more incense to Lucifer, as a seeker of the Royal Secret. Then, as the next part of the initiation he had made his final vow, so that he could receive the 32nd degree Master's Luciferian baptism.

He had vowed: *"I do most solemnly vow and promise, that I will be until I die the implacable enemy of all spiritual tyranny, over souls and consciences of men, resisting all claims of church, synagogue, and mosque to outlaw free conscience and enslave thought and opinion, and compel men to believe what it may prescribe."* In so doing, he had disavowed the Bible as well as the Quran and all other scriptures and pledged himself to the pursuit of light in the Luciferian religion. Montague immediately received a powerful anointing that swept over him, pinning him to the floor; for several minutes, he was unable to move and he had heard words spoken in a strange language, an ancient tongue, and new spiritual gifts were embedded in his soul. The voices had remained within him.

From that day forward, he saw himself with a new perspective, somewhat divine in nature, and superior to the ordinary men, who in his view were little more than cattle. So today, he looked forward with eager anticipation to receiving even more powers as he progressed to the 33rd degree, and after that, who knew? In his heart, he had always known that this was to be his destiny, to ascend above every other, to rule under

Lucifer at the highest level. The Union of the Americas would be under his hand, he would outshine the other Masters of the Temple, he would be selected for rapid advancement above his fellows; tomorrow couldn't come soon enough! He threw a handful of incense upon the eternal flame and prostrated himself once more before the image of Lucifer. He offered his prayers in the strange Persian tongue of Mithraism, which is the worship of Mithra, another name of Lucifer, and he performed his rituals as he had been taught by his instructors.

David had been given an address out at Silver Spring; it was in a quiet old neighborhood of New Washington that was predominantly Jewish. He was told to look for a brownstone house with a black gate; the house was almost opposite the synagogue called Tifereth Israel Congregation. The street address was given as 7701, 16th Street NW, but the synagogue was actually at the center of the block north of Juniper Street, North West. He had decided to drive himself and Nick tagged along; with an eye to security, they thought it best not to leave the vehicle unattended. The late morning traffic was still light and they had made good time down the Capital Beltway. They had selected the upper deck of the freeway because most travelers were unwilling to pay the additional tolls, but David preferred to save themselves the hassle of navigating the commercial traffic on the lower decks.

David's comm. link rang, it was Rick Blade. "David, this is Rick. Look, James asked me to keep an eye on you and we have been shadowing you since you left Northside Dome. I want you to know that you have picked up a tail. Someone must have been following James and picked you up when you left Duane's residence. Don't go directly to your appointment, take the scenic route if you like, you might stop off in one of the parks. We shall take care of the tail, but wait for my all clear before approaching the Silver Spring district. Is that clear?"

"OK, hearing you loud and clear. If I reach 16th Street North West without hearing from you, we will just drive down until we find the turn off for Rock Creek Park, it's big enough to attract sightseers and we won't seem out of place if we park in a recreational area."

"Good, it sounds as if you are getting used to this cloak and dagger stuff! I'll be in touch soon."

David had no doubt that his tail would soon be having an unfortunate traffic accident. He'd be better off dead than being interrogated by Rick Blade's operatives. Fifteen minutes later he received a text, 'safe to proceed', Rick had got his man!

The directions to Arnold Nobel's brownstone were sufficient and they parked the ground car down the street from the house. They had agreed that Nick would keep a watch on the street while David conducted the interview. He would alert David if hostiles appeared in the neighborhood, and Rick's team wouldn't be far away too.

The door opened at David's first knock, and an elderly rabbi looked at him suspiciously through the narrow opening of the door. "State your name, please." He said in a heavy foreign accent.

"My name is David Mackintosh, and Duane sent me. He said to tell you, Mount Olympus." The elderly man opened the door wider.

"Then, come in Douad, come in." He said

"Why did you call me Douad, sir? My name is David."

"Same thing," he replied, "in the Middle East we say Daoud. Now you should know that I have to leave here soon. They are looking for me you know. Did you take precautions against being followed?"

"Yes, we took precautions, and the tail was taken care of. There is nothing to lead anyone to you. So, if you are in a hurry we will get straight to the point."

"Quite, quite." The old man replied, "Please excuse my rudeness. We shall not conduct our discussion in the hallway, shall we?" He tittered. "Follow me Douad; we shall sit in the study."

He led the way down the shadowy hallway; there was a strong smell of boiling cabbage coming from the kitchen and the house reeked of it, and cats. There were cats everywhere, David counted at least five. They regarded him with the disdain for strangers that is peculiar to the breed, and watched him from the corners of the study; a ginger one looked down from the top of the bookcase.

"Do you like tea or coffee, David? I am partial to tea myself. I drink it in the Middle Eastern manner, with cardamom. I prepared some just now; I thought that you would be on time." He didn't wait for David's reply, but poured two narrow glass cups for them. "We call this 'chai', it's very good for the health, they say. I hope that you don't mind the sugar, I premix it with sugar as I'm fond of sweet tea."

David sipped at his tea. It was very sweet, but with the cardamom it was nice. He looked around the study, it was a working room, piles of papers were arranged neatly along Arnold's desktop, and the shelves of the bookcase were full of books. Some of the books were very old, and the bindings were beginning to split, a few were leather-bound and carried titles in Hebrew or Arabic. David's Arabic was rudimentary but they seemed to be religious works. There were some in English; the titles indicated that they were books about the occult and freemasonry.

Arnold spoke, and startled David from his reverie, "You are looking at a lifetime's work, my boy, wasted years for the most part. But all of this could disappear in a moment, strike a match and poof! What would this man's years have to show then? But, thanks to the wonders of modern technology, we have preserved it all. Take these data crystals. They contain priceless archives of these tomes, and it is a unique record of what I have discovered about the secrets of freemasonry and the Dark Powers behind and above it. Let us begin at the beginning, with me first." David nodded, this was going to be easier than he had expected, the old man had prepared himself well, and the archives were an unexpected bonus.

"You may have been surprised to see that I am a Jew. Actually, I am a Messianic Jew. I have merely returned to my roots, but formerly when I was a freemason, no one knew of my family's Jewish roots and in my blindness, I had despised my roots. Now it serves as an identity that they would never expect me to adopt, but I have little expectation that I will live out the fullness of my years."

David asked, "Sir, tell me about freemasonry, I was told that you attained the thirty second degree, so tell me about the secret agenda of the Illuminati."

"Freemasonry is not a western invention, you know." Arnold replied, obliquely. He clearly preferred to follow his own leading for the interview. "It may well be derived from the most ancient of religions. Let us get our terms of reference sorted out first. The roots of freemasonry are intertwined with and owe a debt to Islamic mysticism and the worship of the gods of ancient Persia. Many historians and authors have neglected the connection between the freemasons with the Moors of North Africa. These facts are clearly presented in the records that I have entrusted with you. I have written a book exposing the truth about Freemasonry and the plans of the higher orders. Why do you think that it was the Kingdom of Morocco in 1777 that was the first nation to recognize the sovereignty of the United States? The beliefs of the Founding Fathers were Masonic, derived from Moorish teachers who had passed on their enlightenment to Europe first and then to America."

He fixed an antique pair of pince-nez and then he reached across the desk and extracted some documents that he had indexed, "See here are some authorities to support my words. Gerard Encausse, a famous 19th century French writer on the esoteric sciences, wrote *'the Gnostic sects, the Arabs, Alchemists, Templars form a chain transmitting ancient wisdom to the West. This explains why within the Ritual of Freemasonry there is the admission "we came from the East and proceeded to the West."'* Here too, a Masonic author Bernard H. Springett says: *'The plain fact that much of what we now look upon almost entirely as Freemasonry has been practiced as part and parcel of the religions of the Middle East for many thousands of years, lies open for anyone who cares to stop and read, instead of running by. But it is frequently and scornfully rejected by the average Masonic student...'*"

"So, Arnold, please excuse my interruption, you have satisfied me of Freemasonry's eastern roots. What else did the Masons bring to America?"

"I will not go into the history of the Founding Fathers; so many authors have dwelt on such questions as, for example, why did the layout of the city of Washington D.C. incorporate the pentagram? The answer is self-evident: it was designed by Freemasons, as was the former U.S. Dollar bill and the Great Seal of the United States – all packed with freemasonry symbolism. The symbol on the reverse of the old U.S. dollar bill has reemerged on the new currency of the Union of the Americas, thus proving that the Illuminati are still pulling the strings. Now, let us consider that pyramid. It is actually a trapezoid, completed only by the capstone, which is the 'all-seeing eye' of Lucifer himself. There are thirteen stages in the base of the pyramid; they comprise degrees of power in the freemasons' society. Thirteen is a significant number in Freemasonry and Luciferian numerology. Beginning at the bottom and ascending, the first three degrees are called the Blue Lodge, then under the Union of the Americas we have the Orders of the Scottish Rite or York Rite Masonry, The Shrine, Grand Sovereign Inspectors General – 33rd Degree Supreme Council of Grand and the Sovereign Inspectors General. Then the higher divisions fall under the European or Esoteric Masonry: the order of the Trapezoid, the Ancient & Primitive Rite (of 97 Degrees), the Satanic cult of Ordo Templi Orientis (which is often referred to by its initials, O.T.O.), The Palladium, The Illuminati, The 9 "Unknown Men", The "Seven" and finally, the supreme head of the pyramid, The Great Architect of the Universe or Ain Soph Aur, who has Light without limit. You will note that the pyramid has thirteen levels of enlightenment, and there are thirteen orders of the secret society."

"Since these are degrees of enlightenment, do all members realize the nature of this beast?"

"That is an interesting choice of word. Lucifer is a beast, though he portrays himself as an angel of light, no to be more exact, as the God of light. But to answer your question, David, the answer is no. One of the great thinkers of freemasonry, founder of the Scottish Rite and author of several documents about freemasonry was called Albert Pike. Pike instructed them to use the name 'God' in the presence of the lower degree members, but the higher degrees of thirty to thirty three, do know that 'God' means Lucifer. These poor fools of lower degree believe that they are serving a Christian organization. *It is not and never has been Christian.* It is Luciferian, as Pike was openly a practicing Luciferian. Lucifer has various names, like Mitra, which means -- The fire, the dawn, or the morning star. Lucifer, not Yeshua or Jesus, is the god of freemasonry. Lucifer hijacked the title of Yeshua, who scripture calls the 'morning star', while Lucifer is called only the 'son of the morning'. Freemasonry in the higher degrees worship Lucifer plainly and this is called the 'Royal Secret', it is secret from even their own junior members!"

"Now a few moments ago when you listed the thirteen stages to enlightenment, you mentioned two orders of men above that of the Illuminati. I had always thought that the Illuminati were the top dogs?"

"Dogs they may well be, but they are not the *top* dogs. The illuminati are like the Board of Directors in a company. Above them, there is a Managing Director, which corresponds to the Nine Unknown Men; then you have the Vice Chairman of the Board, which would be the 'Seven', and then there is the Chairman who is Satan or Lucifer as he prefers to be called. These men are steeped in evil, totally corrupt and well versed in all powers of witchcraft, and most of them also practice Satanism. They are hidden from the world, but prefer to orchestrate the world's crises to bring about the plan of Lucifer. These men's ancestors each passed on the Craft to the succeeding generation within their houses, so they have been around for millennia; and as you look at the world about us, who can doubt that they are achieving their goal? Their goal is a One World Government and a One World Religion, all under Lucifer's control."

"Arnold, I noted that you used the term 'The Craft', I thought that this was confined to practitioners of witchcraft. Can you explain that?"

"Yes, I can. You see, Lucifer's kingdom incorporates many practices that deny the one true God, Yahweh. There are the false religions and cults too, they abound. But in the Luciferian religion they are blended together. Elements from all of these paths of error are to be found in Luciferianism. The same demons that inhabit witches also possess Satanists and the practices of the Ordo Templi Orientis are almost indistinguishable from those of The Church of Satan and other satanic worshiping groups. Satan is the author of confusion, and it is easy to see that by this strategy he has sucked in many souls who would otherwise have initially rejected him."

"Ok, thank you for clarifying that point. I can see why researchers have likened this field to Hercules' second labor."

"Oh, do you know the story about the Lernean Hydra?" David shook his head.

"Well, it is just a story of course, a myth. But probably there might have been a large water snake that Hercules was asked to kill. The difficulty was that when he cut off a head, two more would grow back in its place. In the myth, the Hydra had nine heads, one of which was immortal. No one knew which one it was unfortunately. But Hercules had a plan, together with his nephew, Iolas, he would cut off a head and Iolas would immediately cauterize the monster's neck with a flaming torch, so that the heads could not grow back. Eventually, all of the heads were cut off and the monster died. Take this as an allegory for your mighty labor, Douad. Your namesake also destroyed a monster, Goliath. He also was full of blasphemy and pride, but in the end his head was also cut off. You have to do likewise! Cut off the heads of the Illuminati and the body of the monster will die."

"Thank you Arnold, we are going to do just that. I'm sorry but I have taken much of your time, and can see that you are tiring now. Let me ask you one final question. Since you had attained the 32nd degree and could have been permitted to ascend higher, you must have gleaned some understanding about what is their weakness, what do they fear most?"

"The answer to your question is simple. Their kingdom is a kingdom of *fear*; of betrayal and punishment. Fear permeates every facet of the life of witches, wizards, masons of high degree and even Satan himself, for he fears the Lake of fire; he knows that it is coming, and this is his greatest deception upon his followers. Those who serve him believe his lies, receive his gold and power and all that this world has to offer, but in his heart Satan lives in fear, and he conceals this from his followers, knowing that they will precede him into that lake of fire. So my answer is: *fear*, use fear to defeat them!"

David thanked the old man and let himself out. Arnold Nobel sat quietly in his study. He reached for his Hebrew Bible and read with consolation the words of the prophet, in the Book of Isaiah, Chapter 66, verses 22 to 24:

For as the new heaven and the new earth which I will make will be forever before me, says the Lord, so will your seed and your name be forever. And it will be, that from new moon to new moon, and from Sabbath to Sabbath, all flesh will come to give worship before me, says the Lord. And they will go out to see the dead bodies of the men who have done evil against me: for their worm will ever be living, and their fire will never be put out, and they will be a thing of fear to all flesh.

Chapter 10

"Princes and Nations shall disappear from the face of the Earth ... and this Revolution shall be the work of Secret Societies." Adam Weishaupt: *Discourse for the Mysteries*

As James walked to his vehicle, he was receiving messages on his comm. link from Rick who hovered about him like a guardian angel. "James, we have identified one man in a red car. He may well have backup, so let's get them all lined up. We have checked your vehicle and it is clean, well it is now. We removed an explosive device which was attached to the wheel and an electronic bug from the bodywork. Just drive slowly down the highway, as if you were on your way to the office. When you reach the main intersection, do an unexpected u-turn. They will have to follow suit and we will pick up the rear tail first and then the one nearest to you. If necessary, we will repeat a couple of times. We will interrogate them at a safe house."

James drove off at a sedate pace. Rick's team saw the red car follow him and then shortly after, a white car pulled out and joined the procession downtown. When Rick was satisfied that there was just the two cars, he had two cars box in the white car, while a light truck rammed the red car amidships. With guns drawn, the operatives surrounded both cars and the drivers surrendered. James returned to see what type of fish they had caught in their net.

The driver of the first car was a local black gang member, and he knew nothing. He protested his innocence until one of Rick's operatives educated him with a knee to the groin. After that he was more forthcoming: he had been hired by a guy from Central America, and he was supposed to report on James' movements throughout the day. The operatives frisked him and liberated some weapons from his person and the trunk of his car. He also had a street photograph of James pinned to the dashboard of his car. He was led off protesting, his hands tied behind his back with plastic restraints. The other car was a different matter. Agents surrounded the car with guns leveled. The trunk of the car was forced open and the agents found that it contained a sniper's rifle, several automatic weapons and some explosives. There were two Hispanic males inside, both carried diplomatic papers from a Central American country and sat unperturbed when Rick's team flashed police badges at them. The driver spoke up confidently, "Officers, why have you stopped this vehicle? Can't you see that we have diplomatic plates? You have no right to interfere with us and that search of our trunk is a crime against international diplomatic law." By way of an answer, Rick pulled him out of the car by his hair, while one of his men grabbed the second man. "How dare you? Release us immediately!" The first diplomat shouted angrily, "I shall report this matter to the Ambassador. I'll have your badge for this."

Rick's colleague looked questioningly at Rick, and Rick nodded. "You are both terrorists, we're taking you in for questioning under the martial law of the Union. You have no rights under that law. We shall check if these diplomatic ID's are genuine or not." The agents slammed them down face first and unnecessarily hard onto the bonnet of their car. A moment later, both of the diplomats were handcuffed and hooded, before being unceremoniously shoved into the back of a van.

They were driven off, still shouting, but the police siren deterred any curious bystanders from interfering.

The now unmarked van drove up to the electronically operated gates of the safe house, which was in a residential area of Mount Pleasant. In such neighborhoods and such times as these, people kept to themselves and the sign on the outside of the gate read, 'Mental Rehabilitation Center'. The neighbors were used to comings and goings at all hours, and a bit of shouting would be put down to one of the residents having a bit of a fit. The diplomats were hustled through the side door and dragged downstairs where interrogation rooms awaited them.

Rick had found that some of the old techniques often worked quicker, so in adjacent rooms, the prisoners were put through some vigorous water-boarding, followed by some vicious slaps across the face. No questions were asked initially, and the interrogators worked on them silently but methodically, ignoring the screams of the two prisoners. The men had initially tried to play it tough and both had vowed that they would never give up any information; but the incessant torture began to weaken them and eventually through their tears, they cried out, asking their interrogators what they wanted to know.

James chose prisoner number one. He asked him the obvious questions first: why were you following me, and who sent you "? There was a deafening silence and, in the adjacent room, Rick got the same response. They continued the softening up treatment for a few more minutes. Then Rick fired his gun near to the second man's head and he screamed. The sound was heard in the next room, which was intended.

"W... what was that?" Prisoner number one asked in horror.

"Oh, he refused to cooperate. We can't wait about all day. We shot him. Now, about my questions?" James replied, in a matter of fact sort of way. The man began to talk.

They were full time, low level employees and ran drugs and did other jobs for the First Secretary of the Embassy. The First Secretary had instructed them to follow a FBI Special Agent, James Duncan. They had been given full details of his routine, where he lived and worked. They had not been told why James was targeted, just that they were to 'take care of it'. The black guy was the decoy, if anyone spotted the tail, he was supposed to disappear and they would take over. They had fixed an IED on Duncan's vehicle, but, if that failed, then the backup was to shoot him at close quarters as he walked in the street, or in the last extreme, a long range shot with the sniper's rifle that the First Secretary had supplied. The client would pay them all a generous bonus if they finished the job within two days. His name was known only by his initials, M.M. That was about all he could tell James. "Well, it has been nice visiting with you all." James remarked, as he left the room.

James handed him over to Rick. "These men are professional hit men. They know the risks, take out the First Secretary too, he is working for the Olympians; drop them all off at Morgan's gate. I am sure that Morgan will get the message!"

The following morning, three corpses hung by their necks from the ornamental wrought iron gates to Montague Morgan's residence in The Hamptons. His security men claimed that they had seen and heard nothing; Montague fired them all. The incident was unsettling, however, especially in view of the imminent arrival of Herbert Kell. The last thing that Montague wished was that he might be revealed in any weakness. The higher echelons were known to be intolerant of actions that might reveal them, and they took drastic action upon anyone who failed in this regard. Drastic meant a long, lingering and painful death. Morgan felt a stab of fear in his gut. Just the thought of Kell was enough to get his bowels moving, he dashed for the bathroom.

He returned to his basement shrine, and prostrated himself again before Mitra's image. The smoke from the incense burner filled the darkened room as he prayed with all his might. Then a luminescence began to appear about the statue and he heard voices speaking in the ancient language. He discerned that they were warning him that he was in great danger. The face of a strange man appeared before him in a vision, but his eyes flashed with a strange light and his face glowed. The voices told him to take care because this man was coming, and he should summon Lucifer's guardians to fight the battle. Montague was torn, one part of him feared the stranger with the glowing eyes, but he also took comfort in his Lord's divine protection. But who was the strange person, was he a demon? Was he an angelic warrior? He had heard that some of the angelic warriors were fearsome. He left the shrine still feeling unsettled and uncharacteristically confused.

But there was still the unresolved issue of James Duncan. The only communication that he had received from his spies, had told him that Duncan had visited the home of a Supreme Court Justice, Duane Richards, in

Markham, Northside. This puzzled Montague. What business would a FBI Special Agent have with such an important person? Had he stumbled onto the American Eagles, was the Judge playing a double game too? The voices within him told him that he was right. He would seek counsel from Herbert Kell about the matter when he arrived. It would indeed be a feather in his cap if he had unearthed their principal adversary! In the meanwhile, he needed to place another hit team into the field. He made some calls.

A few minutes later, he left his home and drove down Sunrise Highway to Meschutt Beach County Park, where his agent had agreed to meet him within the hour. At the north side of the park, there was a quiet road, called Peconic Beach Road; it ran parallel to the beach. Most times during the mornings the road was deserted and there was little through traffic at any time during the day, except on Public Holidays. Montague knew the area well as he had often sailed in Great Peconic Bay in his youth. He chose a solitary bench facing the sea. There were no houses nearby or buildings within the park area, and only the occasional jogger passed through the area. This was as secure a place as he could imagine at such short notice. His agent was late. Montague hated to be kept waiting. He would deduct a fine from the assassin's fee, to teach him a lesson.

Ten minutes after the appointed time, a small grey van approached him and parked fifty yards down the road. A short man in a knee length leather coat got out of the van carrying a black valise; this had to be Montague's appointment. The assassin walked slowly toward Montague, while his eyes traversed the entire area. He scrutinized the beachfront and the parkland behind where Montague sat. There was nothing to be seen there either, only a small clump of trees that lay about three hundred feet away. Seemingly satisfied, he walked more quickly to Montague, and joined him on the bench, but all the while his eyes swept the area. He sat askew, so that he might see better the ground behind them. Finally, he glanced at Montague, and said, "You called me, why drag me out here? You should have come to me in the city, that's where I do business, this inconvenience will cost you five hundred bucks extra."

Montague was unaccustomed to being addressed in this fashion, but the assassin's reputation was fearsome, and he prudently said nothing to provoke his anger. "I have an urgent problem, it can't wait, and it's the kind that you can fix."

"I guessed as much. Do you have the details of the hit?"

"It's not one, but two persons. One is a FBI Special Agent, his name is James Duncan, and in the file is all the information about him. Don't lose it, it's my only copy. The other is a Supreme Court Justice, Duane Richards, he lives in New Washington also, in Markham, Northside Dome. I need both of them eliminated, quickly and efficiently. I will double your usual fee if you can kill them both within twenty four hours. I hear that you use a laser rifle, what is your range?"

"You just let me worry about that. Did you bring the money? I only work cash up front, and I guarantee success."

Montague reluctantly opened his briefcase handed over a large bundle in untraceable notes, wrapped in a cloth. It was the whole amount of the two fees, so much for his plan to deduct a late fee. This man was a serious contractor, perhaps it'd be better not to mess with him!"

The assassin opened his mouth to say something else, but he never got to say it. Blood splattered over Montague as the assassin's head exploded as the sniper's round found its mark. For a second, Montague froze, horrified and then instinct kicked in, and he ran stumbling and weaving down the road towards his car. Two more bullets whistled past his head and fear lent strength to his legs as he sprinted as hard as he could to the shelter of the car. A third bullet struck his windscreen as he threw the car into reverse and gunned it down Peconic Beach Road. At the western end of the road there is a sharp bend and he screwed the car around it with a swerve and then straightening up, he accelerated away from the area to safety. His heart was thumping and sweat poured from his brow. He put up his hand to wipe it away, but his hand came back covered in blood, he had been hit!

A man walked casually across to the bench and picked up the files, the cash and the data crystal. He spoke on his comm. link, "It's OK Boss, I have the information package and the sound recording, plus his fingerprints are all over them; these should be sufficient to convict Morgan of conspiracy to murder. We are doing the cleanup even as I speak." A white van had pulled up alongside the speaker and a team of four men sprang out and bagged the assassin's corpse. A moment later, a portable hose washed off the blood from the seat and there was no trace to be seen. It took two minutes and there was only a puddle of water left. A jogger passed by but paid no attention to the van, as she was watching a holo-vid on her headset.

Montague Morgan had barely been able to clean himself up before there was a message from the gatehouse that some police officers wished to speak with him. He fixed a Band-Aid over the small superficial cut on his forehead, so much blood from a wound caused by flying glass! He quickly changed his bloodied clothes and emerged in a pristine all in one suit, and felt ready to deal with the cops. What a nerve they had? Didn't they know who he was? They ought to be talking with his butler, about minor matters, not him.

There were two detectives waiting downstairs. They looked like the stereotype flatfoots, broad-shouldered, cheap suits and cold eyes. They didn't offer their hands, but the elder of the pair said abruptly, "Montague Morgan, we would like you to come down to the Police Headquarters, to answer some questions. You have the right to have your attorney present at the interview. Please make your call now, or you will have to wait longer if you call from the station."

Montague felt that confusion sweeping over him again. "What did you say? Why on earth should I go down to your Headquarters, and to answer questions, what's this all about?"

"Sir, you must be aware that under the Emergency Powers, I am not obligated to give you any explanation, or to offer you an attorney. I am being nice to you, understand? So make your mind up what you want to do. You are being questioned in connection with a conspiracy matter. Since you have refused to cooperate, these officers will place you in handcuffs and you will be forcibly taken to the Station."

As he was being frog-marched to the door, he yelled to his butler over his shoulder, "call my lawyer, send him to the Long island Police Headquarters!"

David Macintosh joined Nick in the car. "Any developments Buddy?" he asked as he slid into the passenger seat.

Nick shook his head, "No, everything has been real quiet here. Rick called though a few minutes ago, on your comm. link, it seems that Montague Morgan is being taken in for questioning by the Long Island cops. Apparently, he was recorded whilst he was holding a conversation with an assassin for hire. There is enough evidence to substantiate charges being brought, but it will be a minor problem since the assassin met with an untimely accident. It seems that he swallowed some lead! The main point of the exercise is to warn Morgan off, but having formal charges brought against him will seriously embarrass him. It will also be interesting to see which senior police officer applies pressure to have him released. These Illuminati people hate to be in the spotlight, and it might prejudice his promotion prospects at the least. So, in the wide world it has been busy. How did your meeting go?"

"Hmm, not quite sure what to make of him. He looks like someone's great-grandfather; it's hard to believe that he was once a very high member of the Illuminati. Now he lives alone with his cats and his books. He is also afraid that they will find him and kill him because he has betrayed their secrets, so he is moving soon. I expect that his Hassidic Jewish appearance is a good cover, but he feels that they might be closing in on him. I hope they don't catch him; I quite liked the old boy. Look, while you drive, I want to skim through what he has given to me. He's written a book and he has digitized his entire library; he has entrusted it all to the American Eagles. I suppose that the Olympians would torch it all, and some of those books might be rare because they seemed to be very old."

"No sweat, Dave, I'll stop off somewhere on the way back so you can read in peace. Are we going to our place or Duane's?"

"No, not Duane's. I want to read some of this stuff first, and then we will call him for an appointment. I think that he must be taking some local vacation, because he does seem to be home a lot these days."

"Yeh, well who's gonna fire him anyway? His Boss went on permanent vacation, or so I hear!" They laughed.

Montague was more than irritated, this was *most* embarrassing! How did the Police get evidence of a conspiracy against him? They must have concocted something against him. He'd have his attorney call the Police Commissioner; they'd soon get this sorted out. No one puts a Morgan in security restraints! And how did the newsmen get onto the story so fast? And those cameramen, sticking their lens and video recorders in his face! The cops were no help at all; in fact, he was sure that he had seen the two detectives laughing with the news anchor of the All-American News. In a way it was a relief to climb into the back of the police wagon, but it evaporated when he remembered that the news clip would soon be aired and everyone, including Herbert Kell, would know that he had been exposed. The drive to the Long Island Police Headquarters seemed interminable, and the back of the vehicle smelled strongly of puke, they must have used it to carry some drunks last night. Oh, it was so sickening; he could feel the bile rising up in his throat! He vomited on the floor.

When the police wagon arrived at the station, they helped him out, but no one assisted him to clean his face, so he was forced to walk inside with vomit that had already dried across his chin. This had to be an all-time low for me, Montague reflected miserably.

A burly sergeant conducted him to a holding cell, where his restraints were removed. "You just wait here, Mr. Morgan, your attorney will be down to see you in a few minutes, he's speaking with the Lieutenant at the moment."

The holding cell was clean, but the other two occupants were not. They stank of booze and sweat. Montague could feel the bile rising again, and he forced it back. The bigger of the two was a huge black man; he was dressed in some outlandish clothes that looked like they had come from someone's rag bin. "What you looking at, you little snot?" he asked in a hostile tone.

"Beats me!" Montague retorted. That smart-assed reply only made the black guy madder, and he advanced across the cell and lifting him up from the floor with his right hand he bitch-slapped him three times with his left, before throwing him to the floor. Whereupon the smaller man jumped on him and rained blows and kicks upon Montague, who lay helpless in a ball. "Please leave me alone, I'm sorry," Montague pleaded, but his assailant continued to beat him up.

Finally, the big guy said, "OK, that's enough. We've made our point, now leave him!" The smaller guy, gave Montague one last kick in the ribs, and there was a snap. Something had broken.

"Oh, God! Is this the world that we have created? A world full of senseless brutes, like these?" Montague hung his head and wept. In this world he was like a fish out of water.

A minute later, there was the sound of footsteps and the sergeant returned with Montague's attorney, Clayton Fisk, at his side. "My God! What happened to you? Sergeant, this is Police brutality, I'll sue you ass off for this!" Clayton exclaimed, "Get him out of here, right now!"

"No, he was alright when I put him in here, ten minutes ago. Did you guys do this?" he addressed the other prisoners.

The small guy replied with a sneer, "Nah, he slipped. Just there, see there's a wet patch on the floor." He indicated the spot where Montague's tears had pooled.

The sergeant decided not to press the point. It was their word against Montague's in the end. Montague was escorted upstairs to the interview room and the Sergeant left them alone for five minutes to confer. A moment later, he reappeared with a bowl of water, a flannel and a towel for Montague to clean himself up. Then he left them again.

As soon as the door had closed behind him, Clayton rounded on Montague. "Morgan, what the hell have you got yourself into? They are about to file conspiracy charges against you."

Montague dabbed at the cuts on his forehead and wiped the dirt from his face as he replied, "Oh, that Bank takeover? I can explain all of that."

"Bank takeover? No, this is about conspiracy to commit murder. And one of the victims is a sitting Supreme Court Justice. Now how stupid is that?"

Montague sat paralysed by fear and shock. How on earth had they managed to get evidence on him for the Peconic Beach Road appointment? And how had it happened so fast? "Tell me what evidence they have," he ordered. "They must have something."

"Indeed they do: they have you on tape agreeing to pay an assassin to murder a Judge, Duane Richards, who is the most senior judge in the country; they also have you asking him to kill Special Agent James Duncan; and to cap it all they have your file which lists all of the details about the two victims, presumably when they take your fingerprints that will nail the case down! On top of all that, your briefcase was found on Peconic Beach Road, the cops say that there are some incriminating letters inside it. I can deal with the briefcase because someone else might have planted those documents, but we don't want such publicity, not with Herbert Kell in town today. You have screwed up big time!"

Montague held his head in his hands. He had to think. What about the assassin's body? "Did they say anything about a body?"

"No, no one mentioned a body. Why should they? Is there something that I should know Montague? I'm your lawyer; anything that you say to me is privileged information. I'm also a brother in the Masons, so I'm on your side."

Montague was well aware how that worked: dog eats dog, and only the fittest survive; yes, his worst nightmare would begin if he bared his soul to this brother. "From what you tell me, I see only circumstantial evidence. Where is the person that I allegedly tried to hire? We will tell them that this was a drama scene that we were rehearsing. The cash was with me because I was going shopping this morning, someone must have stolen everything, including my briefcase, from my car whilst I was in the store. It was very careless of me to leave it in an unlocked car, but there is no evidence that a crime was ever committed."

Clayton Fisk shook his head. "Even I don't believe you. But if that is your story, then so be it. I will try to stop this before they can bring charges. You will stay here, and don't give them your fingerprints and don't give a statement until I say so. Are we clear?"

Montague nodded wearily. "Do you think you could arrange a drink for me, water or coffee, anything would do?"

Clayton stood up and nodded. He headed for the door, "I'm going to go over the Lieutenants head. The Commissioner is one of us. He'll stop this in its tracks.'"

Five minutes passed, and a drone entered bearing a tray with a small sealed bottle of water and a cup of steaming coffee. The water was cold and Montague drank it greedily. He was so dehydrated. The coffee was awful, but he drank it anyway. He needed the sugar to boost his energy levels. Ten more minutes passed. and Clayton returned. "It's over," he announced, "but they are holding on to the files because they say that this is private information that you have no right to be holding. Here is your cash, I've signed for it already. Now we can go. Your car is waiting outside. The limousine seems to be all shot up, what happened to that?"

"Some kids from a gang when I was down in New York. I only left it for a few minutes and when I returned it was full of holes."

Clayton gave him another dubious look and said wryly, "Funny how all of these things happened to you when you left your limo unattended." Clayton then added sarcastically, "I'd get another bodyguard, if I were you."

"Yes," said Clayton, "and I just might do that." He added grimly.

Chapter 11

David looked up from the reader. "Wow! I've just come across what must surely be the most evil document ever written. Arnold makes frequent references to it in his book. He says that the authorship implied by its title is a fraud, but it really lays bare the nature of the whole rotten Luciferian organization. It's called *The Protocols of the Learned Elders of Zion,* and it has been denounced by a Christian author called William Guy Carr. Arnold quoted Carr frequently in his book, and his writings were dynamite! Carr, who was a Christian, affirmed that the true author of *The Protocols of the Learned Elders of Zion* was probably a man named Albert Pike, who was a 33rd degree Freemason, a satanist and a Luciferian. The document was intended to discredit the Jews and bring about their destruction. But more than this, the document contained many doctrinal statements about the Luciferian religion and its connection with the New World Order and The Olympians."

"Did Carr explain about the New World Order?"

"Well he did a thorough job of tracing the history of the concept. According to Carr, for the past five thousand years, Lucifer or Satan as he is also known has been working to this end: a One World Government and a One World Religion. He raised a shadowy group of men to mastermind the project, Nobel calls them The Synagogue of Satan, and their calling has been passed on from one generation to the next in the same super-wealthy families. He also lists major banks that act as front organizations for the Olympians. This group of top echelon Luciferians consists of 39 men who secretly run the world today, just as their ancestors did before them for hundreds of years. Gradually the world system was conformed to the pattern that they have worked patiently toward. According to Carr, even a hundred and fifty years ago, all over the world they ran the financial systems, the legal systems and the political administrations, and they still do, it seems. Eventually, they plan to openly declare themselves, but I'm afraid by that time it will be too late to stop them. Already we are well on that road in the Union of the Americas, let's hope that Duane's wonder protein can do all that he is hoping for it."

"Is this the same stuff that Dr. John talked about when we were with him in Sioux Falls?"

"Yes, Nick, and much as it grieves me to withhold facts from you, Duane has asked me not to tell anyone more than what you know already. Sorry about that!"

"No, don't apologize. You gave your word and that is good enough for me. Now about the research data, I don't suppose we shall learn much about the present hierarchy of the Illuminati today, but it would help us if we knew their game plan. When and where were these 'Protocols' printed?"

"They were originally published in 1905 under a different title, I think in Russia, and then reissued as the Protocols. They were delivered as a series of open lectures to students of the occult society, but you have to realize that even to their own followers they were deceptively misstated. For example, the final lecture was omitted. The information contained in it, which identified Lucifer as the mastermind behind the conspiracy, was reserved for only those who were members of the highest degrees.

As I read through these documents, I shall have to weigh everything most carefully. Since it is known that these writings deceived even their own followers, we must expect that they have employed double entendre with certain words and phrases. Carr also promised that if we did our study of the texts in a forensic way, we shall discover that *The Protocols of the Learned Elders of Zion* contains many horrible truths about the secret agenda of a sinister group of powerful figures that have manipulated the world for centuries. Where did Zbigniew Brzezinski obtain his inspiration for the Robotoids, which he revealed in his book *The Technocratic Age*? It was in this evil document, *The Protocols of the Learned Elders of Zion,* that it mentions the creation of human cattle to serve the Elite class. Thus the creation of the Robotoids, which we have seen with our own eyes, was the objective of Luciferian policy as long ago as 1776, and it was written for the guidance of the Olympians of today and the Synagogue of Satan that rules over them. In *The Protocols of the Learned Elders of Zion* we also find it stated that they intend to commit genocide on an unprecedented scale: two thirds of the population of the world! This is what is just down the road for us, if we don't stop them now. The urgency of the hour is great, but if we do not act, the fate of humanity will be dire indeed."

"Wow! David, you have already discovered some very disturbing policies. We have a duty to bring this before the people. Let's get back to base to start work without any delay!"

A sleek, black executive stratos jet hovered before maneuvering to land in a discreet corner of the New York Sanchez International Airport. The jet bore no logo to identify it, as befitting a diplomatic VIP's transportation. The landing area was cordoned off by a ring of Secret Service agents and armed security guards. Near the edge of the landing pad, a stretched ground-car limousine with blacked out windows stood awaiting the disembarking VIP. When the jet's doors slid back, a small, dapper gentleman stepped out onto the hydraulic platform that would gently lower him to the ground. The captain of the stratos jet stood waiting to shake his hand in the doorway, but Kell was aloof and ignored the outstretched hand. No one else presumed to be as presumptuous and Herbert Kell turned away to face the outside world. He paused for a long moment surveying the security arrangements. There were no welcoming bands, nor any flags on display; this was a low key visit. But he had been expecting that at least the State Governor would have showed up. Only the Director of the Airport Authority stood nervously waiting to greet the visitor. Herbert Kell ran his fingers through his jet back hair and flicked imaginary dust from his dark grey all in one suit. Seemingly satisfied with the security arrangements, Kell nodded to the attendant and the platform descended. It was a warm spring morning, but the strong men in the security detachment shivered as Kell walked past. He exuded no warmth whatsoever, either in his expression or his demeanor. Having seen the Captain's rebuff, the Airport Director made no attempt to make physical contact, but he addressed Herbert Kell with great respect. "Your Excellency, you are most welcome to our beautiful country. On behalf of the Joint Chiefs of Staff, we wish you a very enjoyable visit."

Kell fixed him with a look that chilled him to the bone and his flow of words ceased. "The representative of the Joint Chiefs of Staff is also not here. Why?"

The Director shook his head helplessly. Then he grasped his throat with both hands and sank to his knees. His face was flushed as he fought for air. He looked pleadingly up at Kell who regarded him with a dispassionate look.

Kell instructed him, "You tell them that I consider this to be an insult." The Director nodded and bowed before Herbert Kell as the grip on his throat was released. "Have you provided all that I requested for my journey?"

"Yes, Your Excellency. It is as you ordered. They are inside the limousine, Excellency."

Herbert Kell walked away from him and went to the limousine where the uniformed chauffeur waited with the side center door open. Two very young girls could be seen inside the limo. They were dressed in party clothes. Herbert Kell entered the limousine and sat down facing the girls. Suddenly his whole demeanor changed, and he beamed a dazzling smile. "Now my precious ones, what nice gift have you brought for me?" One of the girls withdrew a syringe of heroin from the cocktail cabinet, which she expertly injected into a vein in his arm, and then she injected herself. Then the second girl followed suit and both girls began to undress Kell before removing their party dresses also.

The limousine sped from the airport without being stopped at the security gates. Herbert Kell wasn't bound by the laws of any land. The traffic was heavy until they reached the Beltway. They took the upper level and the road was almost clear, so the powerful limousine accelerated and exceeded the speed limits all the way to his hotel, The Waldorf-Astoria Hotel on Park Avenue. Herbert Kell was shown directly to the presidential suite and the two girls - who were not only the daughters of a satanic couple, but also child prostitutes - left with the limousine. They had fallen asleep on the seats, fully under the effects of the narcotic drug.

Kell, however, was only slightly high by that time, his system having gained great tolerance through the regular use of drugs in his private life as well as in the rituals of the Craft. The holo-television in his suite was activated by voice command and he selected a news channel. He expected that it would be the usual trivia to entertain the masses, but things had changed much since his last visit. He was shocked to see real news being broadcast instead of stories of cute dolphins playing with children and suchlike. Then the broadcast went into a review of the day's main headlines and there it was, Montague Morgan's face splashed all over the news. He was being arrested; it appeared that there were charges of conspiracy to assassinate a Supreme Court Justice and a Special Agent of the FBI. This was intolerable! Morgan had broken a cardinal rule, no two: be discreet and don't get caught.

"Yes, it's shocking isn't it?" A voice from the dressing room spoke, but it was in a mocking tone. Kell turned to see who the speaker might be. A middle aged man dressed in a white middle-eastern robe walked casually across the room and chose to recline on the leather sofa in a most relaxed manner. Kell was amazed at the man's effrontery. Didn't this man know whose room he had broken into?

"Yes, of course I do, Herbie!" The man replied as if he had read his thoughts, "And by the way, pedophilia is still a crime in New York. But you will be changing all that soon won't you?"

"Well, since you can read my mind, look at what I'm about to do to you. You made a big mistake coming into this suite, but I fear that you won't live to regret it!"

"Is that so, Herbie? Are you sure about that?" His visitor asked in the same mocking tone. "Well do what you are planning to do, let's get the 'he killed with a look' thing out of the way. Then we will have a real conversation, Mr. Child Molester.''

There was something about the man's quiet confidence that unnerved Herbert Kell; he summoned his demons to strike the man down, but they actually refused, saying, "We can't, he's not a mortal man, he's different!'' Fear stabbed at Kell's heart. This must be the One that The Master had warned him about. And here he was, and he was immune to his weapons. Well perhaps there was a way. He reached into a side pocket and withdrew a small laser pistol. He pointed it at the stranger and fired. And the beam passed straight through the stranger and drilled a hole through the sofa and the wall behind him.

"Oh, that was nice! It gave me quite a buzz. We should do this again sometime. Now, enough tomfoolery, let's get down to men's talk shall we?" The mocking tone was replaced by a coldly serious one. "You sit, no you can kneel. Just over there."

Herbert Kell found no strength in him too resist the voice of the stranger. He felt himself being dragged across the room, but the stranger didn't touch him. He merely stood watching. Kell's knees collapsed and he fell down, with his face forced to look at the carpet, which was only an inch from his face. How he managed to remain in this position, he couldn't tell because his arms were clamped by his sides, and he was powerless to move them.

""Let me go!" He ordered.

"Oh, like this?" The stranger asked, and Kell's nose collided with the floor with all his weight upon it. Kell howled with pain, and blood gushed out of his nose. He was elevated again until his face was tilted up to see the stranger's face. Light flashed out of the stranger's eyes and his whole body now pulsated with light, and his power emanated across the room. Kell screamed in fear.

"Now let's get the doctrine clear first shall we? You worship Lucifer, whom you say is God. You say that Yahweh and Adonai are evil, but Lucifer is good and is working in the cause of humanity. That is pure crap! If Lucifer is good, and you are one of his 39 chosen elite, then your actions would have to be good too. But you are profoundly corrupt and evil, as witness your behavior in the limousine with those two little girls. What were they six or seven years old? It is people such as you who corrupt the innocent. Let me tell you, 'The wages of sin is death', and you have been working hard for your wages for most of your lifetime. What do you have to say for yourself?"

"Don't preach at me, I don't believe any of your lies. In a little while we shall reign over this Earth and we will purify it with blood. Then our Lord Lucifer will sit on his throne forever. But you will never see it, we shall kill you. We have powerful demons at our beck and call, you can't defeat them."

"Maybe, I can't. But you are deceived if you actually believe that the demons are at your beck and call. They serve Satan and they would happily kill you as look at you. But then I am not alone either. Now I want to take you on a little trip, Herbie, seeing as you have come here on a sort of vacation, let's call it a sightseeing trip. Don't worry about the transport; I'll take care of everything." On face value, his words seemed harmless, but there was something menacing about the expression on his face that created a sense of foreboding in Herbert Kell.

A moment later they were far away from New York, on Earth or in some distant place, he couldn't tell, but he was suspended by the scruff of his neck by the stranger, and it was hot, very hot. He looked down and what he saw made him scream. Fear surged through him; he wet himself and soiled his pants. Beneath him, perhaps fifty feet only, a boiling cauldron of what looked like red molten lava hissed and bubbled and spat at him. He pleaded with the stranger not to drop him into that fire, he pleaded as he had never in his life pleaded before. Tears streamed from his eyes, but they evaporated in the sizzling atmosphere above the red hot liquid. He was descending, closer and closer to the flames above the liquid, his clothes were smoldering and his shoes began to burn. "For God's sake save me!" he cried as loud as he could.

""Which god are you calling to, you maggot? Yahweh or Lucifer?"

"To Yahweh, the one true God." He screamed with the utmost desperation. Immediately, he was withdrawn from the fire and he found himself standing in his hotel suite. His clothes were in ruins, mere ashes, and his shoes had lost their soles. All over his body he was burned, probably the scars would remain as a constant reminder. He looked in a mirror. He didn't recognize the face which stared back at him. It was streaked black from the fire, his eyebrows had been burnt off but it was his hair that made him screech with shock, it was totally white!

The stranger stood watching him. "Do you like your new look?" he asked in that same mocking tone. "Are you convinced now? Was Lucifer there to help you? No, he wasn't, but his messengers have told him by now that you denied him, called Yahweh the one true God. You can never return to serve Lucifer. My advice is run away and hide for the remainder of your miserable life! There are no words to describe what I might feel for you, but He whom you called out to has forgiven you, so I can say nothing more, except farewell!" And with that closing salutation he vanished from view. Herbert Kell dashed for the room phone and called reception, he ordered his limousine to take him back to the airport.

Chapter 12

As Herbert Kell scrambled to put as much distance as possible between him and the man with the flashing eyes, a second stratos jet was landing at the New Washington International Airport. On board, a man dressed in the uniform of the British Army sat in the business section of the jet. He was generally known as Lt. Colonel John Ballantyne, but his clandestine cover was Jack Bailey, leader of the UK Angels Network. John worked on the staff of Field Marshal David Miller and the UK's military leadership had given the Angels much logistical support and direction in their battle against the forces of the British dictator, Ian McGregor. John was travelling under diplomatic papers as a courier to Supreme Court Justice Duane Richards and he carried with him a valise that he never let out of his sight. It carried a most precious consignment: three packets of the synthetic form of the Kyoto Protocol protein, also known as KP. Similar missions were in process to all points across the globe. KP was on the move!

The much awaited public announcement from the Joint Chiefs of Staff couldn't have been better timed. It was broadcast throughout the Union on all channels and media at ten o'clock Eastern Time. The announcement was received with a tremendous outpouring of joy by the populace. In every city, throughout the Union, people flocked to the streets to express their relief. Antique weapons were brought out of cupboards and secret storage stashes and dusted off, before the owners rushed out into the streets to fire their weapons in the air; it was euphoria, such as hadn't been seen for three generations. Immediately, the resistance group issued their prepared statements offering a cessation of violence, and called for the military to reciprocate by returning their troops to barracks. A further statement was then issued by the Joint Chiefs promising a full return to civilian rule and asking the population to cooperate during the transition period.

As Lt. Col. John Ballantyne walked through the Arrivals department, he was amazed at the festive atmosphere in the terminal: even the Customs officials were smiling and they waved him through without asking to see his diplomatic papers. A quick glance at his papers by the Immigration desk official and he was through. Duane had come personally to meet him and they shook hands and walked together to his limo which was parked in the VIP parking area. They talked as they walked; small talk about the flight mostly, these were early days for civilian rule still and there would certainly be continuing surveillance of all arriving passengers throughout the Airport terminal. Duane's driver relieved John of his overnight bag and they settled down on the limousine's comfortable seats. John accepted a fruit juice from the bar; it was still too early for a scotch. Duane had a soda. "Here's to freedom, John, and the overthrow of all dictators!"

"I'll gladly drink to that," John replied, and they clinked their glasses.

"So, what is the situation now in UK and Euro Zone?" Duane asked, "Are we all set for the international conference in London? It's very close now, and I must confess that now we have arrived at this critical point in our plans, I'm getting butterflies in my stomach."

"In that you are not alone. As we confirmed in our teleconference the other day, synthetic KP is now in full production and we are dispatching it internationally. Like you in the Union, the other states will produce their own supplies and take care of distribution to the provinces and neighboring small states which lack the facilities to produce their own synthetic KP. David has suggested that we do a coordinated launch of the KP in two weeks. Will this give you sufficient time? We thought that you might be able to manufacture the KP in three regions, say East and West coasts and in the Mid-west, so I have brought you three packets in powder form. The powder is fully soluble and in water it is odorless, tasteless and colorless. It is promised by the chemists that it will be undetectable by the chemical filters in the treatment stations."

"That was most thoughtful of you and David Miller. It will save us a couple of days if we can begin production simultaneously. We have good men in Los Angeles and Sioux Falls; they will know what to do. We shall concentrate on the cities and the detainee camps, as well as the military installations. Are there any observed side effects of KP?"

"Only one, that I know of: it may cause minor nausea in the first three days, and then there is the iris effect, see my eyes." John removed his shades and Duane was startled by his iris' intense blue color. "This is a permanent effect we believe, or at least for as long as the person continues to receive regular dosing of KP. The telepathic awareness in our test subjects began after the third day and they reported a heightened sense of awareness by the seventh day. This is going to make a difference, Duane, believe me.''

"Well here we are at my residence. Will you be staying for just the one night, John? You are most welcome to stay longer if you wish.''

"No, but thank you. There is much to do still in UK, and we are breaking Ian McGregor down daily. We have switched now to open military defiance and the

Army and Air force have been destroying targets which have particular symbolic relevance to McGregor's Defenders. For a long while we were underfunded and poorly equipped, but now we are taking what we need from the Defenders. The Army and Air Force are getting their teeth at last! Why just the other day, Jim Stewart appropriated a Scranton military fighter jet and we put it to good use; we remodeled the front of the Defenders' headquarters too. It's been great payback!''

"You mentioned the name, Jim Stewart. Do I know him?'' Duane asked ingenuously.

"Well, you may have heard of him through his manufacture of scanning equipment. Stewart Scanners are just about ubiquitous. But, Jim also happens to be the father of the three half-Japanese children who carried the KP in their DNA. It was their arrival in England that got the ball rolling. Jim is an interesting person in his own right, quite a character actually. Maybe you will get to meet him sometime.''

"Yes, I'll look forward to that," Duane answered drily. John looked at him sharply.

"Anything I should know?'' he asked perceptively.

"No, not at all. If you don't mind an early lunch, I'd like to get started because we have a busy schedule today. It'll be more on your time zone I suppose too. Let's eat. Bob made a real English meal especially in your honor: roast beef with Yorkshire pudding! It's a bit early for me to eat lunch, but it smells so good, doesn't it?'' Indeed the aroma of the food had wafted into the living room and their taste buds had begun to salivate. They sat down to lunch and Bob poured them a couple of beers, and then he began to carve the joint.

"Duane, there is one other piece of information. We had a tip off that a very prominent member in the Olympians had arrived yesterday in New York. My informant says that he has come to see someone that you are interested in, Montague Morgan. Montague Morgan is the son of the former head of the Olympians. We don't know much more except that the visitor's name is Herbert Kell, he's a Swiss national, and he usually stays at the Waldorf-Astoria Hotel on Park Lane. We suspect that he is a very senior member of the Illuminati and that might explain the visit to see Montague Morgan. All we know about him is that his past is very secretive, but everywhere he goes he is treated like royalty or a head of state. Do you know why he is here? He could be trouble, especially now."

"Let me check. We'll finish lunch and then I'll call my number two, James Duncan. James has his network of agents throughout New York and the rest of the Union, for that matter. If anyone can ferret out the reason, James can."

Bob had surpassed himself and John made a point of going through after lunch into the kitchen to congratulate the old maestro. "Bob, even my mother couldn't have cooked me roast beef with Yorkshire Pudding as good as that. Thank you very much!" Bob seemed actually embarrassed, but he flushed with pleasure.

"You made my labors worthwhile, Sir." He replied humbly. John returned to the living room where he found Duane deep in conversation on his comm. link, he was talking with James and nodding his head as James' report came over. Finally, he hung up and turned to John with a broad smile on his face.

"Well, it's all good news! James has a mole inside Morgan's Temple. The mole informed James that the Illuminati were supposed to have a special initiation of a 33rd degree mason today. It seems that this was the reason for Herbert Kell's visit to New York. Montague Morgan was to receive the initiation and he would have automatically have been officially appointed as the

Illuminati's new head honcho in The Union of The Americas and South America. Now mark this, this Kell is a seriously dangerous man. It is said that he is one of 39 men that oversee the implementation of the New World Order. People like McGregor and the other dictators of Euro Zone are ultimately his pawns. Well, something very strange occurred. James has another man on the reception of the hotel where Kell had a suite. He arrived yesterday, and went straight to the Presidential Suite. At that time, everything seemed normal, but a little later something inexplicable happened. About one hour after he arrived, Kell literally ran out of the Waldorf-Astoria and jumped into his limo and took off for the airport. What is even weirder was that Kell's clothes were in tatters, he smelled as if he had been in a fire, he ran out of the hotel barefoot but his shoes were later found in his room, and they too had been reduced to ashes! Strangely, there was no trace of a fire in the suite. There was a laser burn on the wall also, but no traces of blood were found in the suite. Something else, his hair which had been black as coal, had turned snow white and his face was streaked with soot. James also confirmed that Herbert Kell had immediately left the country in his private jet. Now how is that for a tall story?''

""This beats me in all honesty. One hears of people having a terrible shock which turns their hair white overnight. But in the space of an hour, never! And how does one explain the fire? There has to be a paranormal explanation for this. Aren't all of these guys also into witchcraft and Satanism? Perhaps he dabbled where he shouldn't have and got a lesson to remember?''

Duane nodded pensively; he now had a very good idea who might be able to supply all of the answers to these questions. Instead he changed the subject, "Let me show you to your room, you can freshen up and take some rest. I always find international journeys very tiring, especially with jet lag. We can get together later and we will watch David Mackintosh's latest expose´ on the hidden agenda of the Illuminati. We have timed this to follow on after the rescinding of the State of Emergency. The institutions that have supported the Illuminati will not be able to capitalize on the fluid situation; we shall sweep up all of them and take them down. The one thing that the Illuminati hate is to be put into the spotlight of publicity. David's expose´ is dynamite and it will point the finger at Montague Morgan and his secret order. It will show them as the criminals and traitors that they are."

The courier had delivered a small package to the office of General Abrams. It was marked as "private and confidential", so his aide had not opened it but the package lay next to his in-tray. The General was curious about the package. It was about the size of a wallet, but quite slim. There was no sender's name or address, it simply stated, "By hand Delivery". The Security officer had scanned it and a sticker had been affixed to the package stating that it contained a data crystal but no explosive material. Abrams opened the package with his antique letter knife. Inside the package were a data crystal and a note. He placed the crystal in his reader, but he decided to read the note first. It was written in freehand and in a blue ink, which was uncommon those days.

Dear General Abram,

I am writing this note to alert you to the activities of some members of the Joint Chiefs that are contrary to the plans to return to civilian rule in a democracy. The crystal shows never before seen footage of the training of Robotoid soldiers at several training sites in Nevada and California. The bases are situated in Groom Lake and San Fernando Valley respectively. Note the date and time stamps on the image files. These are current reports. Generals Browning and Fraser are planning a coup and you need to take urgent steps to prevent this before there is any further loss of life.

Signed, a well-wisher

General Abrams was now more than curious; this might confirm the growing suspicions that he had been having about those two. He pressed the play button on the crystal reader.

There were three files listed in the index: "San Fernando Valley", "Groom Lake" and "Miscellaneous broadcasted images". Abram selected the first file.

There was something familiar about the site, then he remembered, there had been a broadcast by the American Eagles showing this site. It had made a powerful impacts as it carried a conversation between some of the guards and Robotoids had been mentioned. This film carried new information about this site. The site sign stated that it was a Water Department facility, but the activity within was definitely of a military character. The site was fenced with a tall wire fence topped with razor wire that curiously faced inward. Small signs within the fence warned that the area was mined and the fence was electrified, but the signs faced inward also. It was clear that the security was more about keeping people in than intruders out. The next scenes showed a large black building about the size of a hangar. Inside the hangar there were hovers and helicopters that carried armaments. Groups of black uniformed men were engaged in armed combat drill and something about the deadly serious expression on their faces told General Abram that these were

Robotoid soldiers. The scene shifted outside where squads of the same soldiers were engaged in target practice with automatic weapons. Other Robotoids were jogging around an obstacle course and they carried heavy packs on their backs.

The next file showed similar activity to that at the San Fernando facility. It opened with Robotoids marching off into the desert in the full heat of the Nevada sun, they too carried heavy pack. The next scene showed a large hangar and there was a most unusual aircraft inside. It seemed to be a triangular shape and the configuration of the body panels told Abrams that this was a stealth aircraft. Why hadn't the Joint Chiefs been told about this aircraft? It looked very sinister, and Abram had no doubt that it was a lethal secret weapon.

The third file showed Robotoids in various locations, some were working in factories, minding machines or moving manufactured goods around; there were shots of brothels with Robotoid whores standing in the streets, and then there were the images taken of the Robotoids storming a blockhouse in a live ammunition exercise. Some of this material had also been broadcast by the American Eagles, but some was fresh according to the date stamps on the film.

General Abram found all of this record to be deeply troubling. He was an Army man; his background was heavy weapons, tanks and suchlike. He had never been involved in the Marines and their 'Special Enforcement' patrols. He was a decent man and he felt both sadness and outrage that such things should be done in the name of the Joint Chiefs. He decided to call Admiral Mendez. "Raymundo, can I send you an urgent package? It is compelling viewing and when you have watched it we have to talk. Please don't talk to Fraser or Browning about this, they are up to their necks in this, and I want your advice about what to do. OK, I appreciate that. My courier will bring it to you personally. Goodbye for now."

He called his aide. "This needs to be copied and kept in my safe. Take the copies across to Admiral Mendez. He's expecting it. Peter, this is very confidential, so hand carry it yourself and only you should deliver it into Admiral Mendez's hands"

The aide took the package and replied, "Leave it to me, sir."

Chapter 13

It had been a poor day yesterday, but Montague was determined that nothing was going to spoil his big day. This was but the first step on his climb to the top of the pyramid. He had heard that the illustrious leaders of the Order were all advanced in years, so Lucifer would soon discard them. He was young and full of zeal, and intensely ambitious: surely his god had noted him and marked him out for higher things. He could hardly contain his rising excitement, oh, the power that would soon be his! He would mete out punishments upon all those who had hindered his plans: that Judge and FBI man would soon feel the wrath as he dispatched demons against them; he had tried using mere men, but soon he would have the spiritual weapons that they couldn't counter. He gloated over their terrible downfall.

He had heard that the Grand master had arrived last night. The Director of the International Airport had called him personally. Montague's power and influence were already being felt in the highest levels and such courtesies reflected the prestige of being such a powerful freemason. But soon, as he ascended even higher, the dread that accompanied his presence would be increased. He had witnessed that fear and trembling wherever Herbert Kell walked and he lusted after the same power for himself.

Herbert Kell was due to arrive in The Hamptons by noon, so Montague had ensured that all of his invited guests would be there to welcome him as befitting his rank. The Temple was dressed with all of the sacred banners and secret animal sacrifices had already been offered in spiritual preparation; Montague had left nothing to chance. He even had a young virgin prepared for the climax of the ceremony. Lucifer would be pleased, he was confident of that. The walls of the Temple were draped in the finest of silks and the banners of all the lodges across The Union of The Americas hung proudly. Around the hall, the Masonic regalia gave the opulent atmosphere that Montague wish to convey to his distinguished principal guest, Grand Master Herbert Kell. First he would place a call to the Grand Master at his hotel, and then he would make one last tour of the Temple to satisfy himself that every little detail was perfect.

Alone in the Temple, he called the Waldorf-Astoria and requested the Presidential Suite. The desk clerk enquired, "To whom did you wish to speak, Mr. Morgan?"

"Why to the occupant of course, His Excellency Herbert Kell."

"Please hold the line, sir.'' He was placed on hold for a moment. Montague was mildly irritated, but he supposed that the Grand Master must be dressing or something.

A new voice came on the line, "Sir, I am the duty manager, how may I help you?''

"Why, I wish to speak immediately to His Excellency Herbert Kell. What is the reason for this delay?''

The duty manager paused before replying, "and you are Mr. Montague Morgan? Yes, I do know you, sir. We do not normally give out information about departing guests, but we can make an exception for you, sir."

"You said, *Departing guests*? You mean to tell me that His Excellency has left? That cannot be! He is supposed to be coming here within the hour; he's coming to my house for a most important function. I have all of my guests waiting for him. Please check your information."

"Well, there is no need for me to check, sir. I personally witnessed him leave the hotel. It caused quite a commotion, I can tell you. He seemed to be in some sort of extreme panic, you might say that he was terrified of something. He was all dirty and his clothes were in tatters, he was barefoot and oh, yes, his hair had turned pure white! Yes, it had turned white during the brief time that he was in his suite. Something *very* strange has happened, sir, there was a laser weapon burn on the wall also, but we found no traces of blood or a struggle. You understand that we respect the privacy of our distinguished guests, and since we had no evidence of a crime, we did not call the police. I do hope that Mr. Kell is alright?"

"Yes, yes," Montague mumbled as his mind reeled. He hung up. What could have happened and where did that leave him now?

"That's a very good question, Montie! I shouldn't let it trouble you though, you have more important things to worry about."

Montague Morgan looked to his side, but his body seemed to be rooted to the spot. He was only able to turn his head. To his horror, the same face he had seen in the vision now appeared beside him. The face was that of a Caucasian, and his hair was snowy white also. His eyes flashed with a bright glow, and Montague became very afraid. This was indeed the same person that his voices had warned him about, but where were his helpers now, just when he needed them?

"Montie, you have been a bad, bad boy!" The man scolded him as if he was a small child. He wagged his index finger of his right hand in the air, but his face carried no suggestion of banter. "My name is Jim, but it doesn't matter really, because you will soon forget it. Please don't waste your energy screaming for help. The doors are locked and I have control over when you will be able to speak. Can you imagine, being locked in your body forever, hearing and understanding everyone around you but unable to communicate? Yes, that is exactly how those poor wretches that you created feel. Of whom am I speaking? Why the Robotoids of course! Deep in their consciousness they know that they are individuals, but you and your kind have robbed them of their ability to live. You reduced them to mere automatons. Today is the day of enlightenment for you all right, but not in the way that you had in mind."

There was something chilling about the words of the stranger who called himself Jim, they seemed superficial, but Montague knew in his heart that beneath the calm voice, Jim was deadly serious. He cried out, but no sound issued from his lips. Even his tears refused to fall. He was trapped in his shell of a body, alone with his voices that were now raised in accusation against him. They reminded him of his failure and accused him of treachery, and they went on and on!

Jim walked in front of him. He held in his hand a large syringe which was filled with a green fluid. Montague's eyes followed the movement of the syringe; he was hypnotized, like a mouse before a snake's eyes. "In this syringe is a cocktail of drugs. They are similar to the drugs that your fellow conspirators shoot into the detainees and other innocents to convert them into Robotoids. I said *similar*, for the drugs are not identical. The Robotoids will recover thanks to a new protein called KP which The American Eagles are even now producing for distribution, but you will not recover. Outside this hall of blasphemy, your guests have also partaken of this drug cocktail. I modified it slightly; it was imbibed with their cocktails. They are all locked in their bodies, just as you will be shortly. But one more thing, in a short time from now, the secret of longevity is going to be discovered. As it happens, it will be by my mother in law. I wanted you and your scum to share in the benefit of this discovery right now, so I've added it to the cocktail. It will extend your life considerably. That will give you an awful long time to commune with your demons and to consider all your wicked ways. Now here is your gift!'' Jim's bantering tone had ceased and his face was filled with a resolve to neutralize the evil plans of this man and his kind.

Montague's eyes were fixed upon the syringe as it moved inexorably towards his brain. Jim administered the drugs directly into the frontal lobe. A single tear escaped and ran down Montague's cheek.

Without waiting to see the drugs' effects upon Montague, Jim walked past him and opened the double doors of the Temple. Outside were two hundred and twenty guests, both men and women, who were dressed in all their finery. These distinguished guests were the cream of the establishment, leaders of society; they were the hierarchy of Satanists, Freemasons, Palladians and other occultists, and they stood like wax figures, only their eyes moved to follow the white robed figure as he strode through the basement reception area towards the stairs. Jim bounded up the stairs and then vanished.

Chapter 14

General Fraser sadly packed away his personal items. His tenure in the New White House had been brief, but he had grown to love the trappings of the Presidential Office. Perhaps he might be able to regain the office through the ballot box, but in his heart he knew that outside of the military he was almost unknown. His brief appearances as the public face of the Junta had given him a taste for the glamor of being a celebrity, but people soon forgot. He hoped that he might be able to influence the advisory panel that were drawing up the guidelines for the new National Reconciliation Tribunal, because he knew in his heart that the atrocities which he had committed would not be easily forgiven or forgotten.

His mind reviewed his options: early retirement with the hope of fading away into obscurity, or entering into a consultancy to influence the new breed of politicians for the new world or perhaps he might proceed with his plans to stage a counter coup? The first went against his nature, he was a pugnacious type, an alpha male, and he was born to lead. The second course was somewhat appealing to the devious side of his personality. A coup, well that was a possible course and one for which he had been preparing for a long time! But would he be able to persuade other senior officers to join him? Browning was in his pocket, but none of the others shared his vision. He would give the matter some consideration, but on the whole he expected that he and Browning would have to go it alone.

His aide called on the intercom. There was a call from General Abrams and Admiral Mendez. They wished to have a conference call. Fraser had a sense of foreboding; these guys had never called him before, not in all the years that he had served on the Joint Chiefs of Staff. He told his aide to lie, to say that he had left the building on some personal business. It was time to get moving!

As he placed his final possessions into a carton, his mind returned to the logistical details of his grab for power. Perhaps he could muster a battalion of Robotoids at Groom Lake and perhaps if he collected all of the dispersed Robotoids into San Fernando, in California, there would be a second battalion. That would have to do for the moment. He passed instructions to his aide, to inform the Los Angeles Area Commander to concentrate his forces in San Fernando. He was confident that once the battalions were assembled in battle order, no one would be able to withstand his advance.

But there was no time to be lost, the raw material for the army was about to be dispersed, they were even now discussing releasing whole camps of detainees, prime stock that would be sufficient for him to form several battalions of shock troops. Such troops could even be trained for operating complex weapons systems. Browning's research labs had even developed fast educational protocols that connected direct into the brain; a soldier could be transformed into a fighter pilot, it would only take a couple of hours, he had been assured. All of the memories and reflexes of a skilled operator could be duplicated in the brain of a Robotoid, it was new technology, but Browning had already proven it in his experimentation laboratories. Yes, this was the best course. He would build an army that no one could defeat!

His aide entered The President's Private Office. "General, do you have any further instructions for me. I mean where are we going, when we leave here?

"Initially, to Edwards Air Force Base. But we shall be moving into the research facility out at Groom Lake. But this information is restricted for now. Understand?''

"Yes, General. Isn't that Area 51?'' General Fraser gave him no answer but stared him down. The aide fled to make the arrangements. The cleaner continued her task, dusting the now empty shelves; she might as well have been part of the furniture because Fraser treated her as such.

In the late twentieth century, the name of Area 51 became synonymous with clandestine operations and research, including it was alleged, captured aliens. General Fraser had never seen any truth in any of those wild stories, but it was the perfect place for conducting his human experimentation project. The military base had been called by various names in its history, such Dreamland, Paradise Ranch and Groom Lake but most recently Homey Airport. One of Area 51's advantages was the restricted airspace around the field that ensured that none of Fraser's colleagues could easily spy on him with terrestrial jets or drones. Indeed, he did not wish to advertise his use of the airbase for his pet highly classified, military Special Access Programs (SAP). In the SAP he was officially developing programs to support the development, testing, and training phases for new weapons systems or research projects, primarily for the Air Force. However, unofficially, Robotoids were being readied to operate the weapon systems for both the Army and the Air Force. Fraser had always known that it might come to this, and instead of transferring the new weapons and technologies to normal Air Force or Army bases, he had stockpiled his men and weapons at Groom Lake.

It is very difficult to keep secret something when some of those who are aware of it do not approve. In this case, the lowly servant in the New White House who was cleaning in the Private Office had overheard General Fraser's conversation with his aide. Unfortunately for General Fraser, she was an embedded agent of the American Eagles and far better educated than her appearance might have suggested, being the holder of a master's degree in computer sciences. She regularly scanned the General's messages for interesting items and she had noted several references to a joint project with General Browning out at 'the Lake'. Knowing that Browning was a scientist, James was very interested to find out more, so he encouraged her to hang around as much as possible in case Fraser let slip a vital detail. It had paid off. She connected the dots; 'the Lake' had to be Groom's Lake, otherwise known as the infamous Area 51.

"This sounds like exactly what David and Nick are good at," James said to himself. He called in a favor and the Director of the FBI made available his personal executive jet to take them to Nevada. Within the hour, they were airborne and their jet touched down in Las Vegas one hour before General Fraser and his party had even made it to the hastily reconstructed Andrews Air Base. A local air taxi service transferred them from Vegas to Alamo, where they were met by one of James' operatives. From there they planned to drive along the Great Basin Highway, which is also known as Interstate 93 and make their way to the small town of Rachel, via Crystal Springs. Rachel was twenty four miles due north of Groom Lake, and it was the nearest town.

General Abrams and his friend Admiral Mendez hadn't believed the aide's story about General Fraser's absence on a personal matter; it was so unlike the man. Then when they learned that he had left the building and was heading for Andrews Air Base, they were sure that he was up to no good. "Raymundo, let's do a little reconnaissance out in California. I have a brigade of heavy armor just outside Los Angeles. I think that we need to do a recce to see for ourselves what's going on at that Water Department." Admiral Mendez agreed, and there was no time to lose.

General Abram contacted his own brigade commander, bypassing the Area Commander who was Fraser's man. "Colonel Davis, you are to investigate this site in the Valley. Send an aerial reconnaissance drone to see what is going on there. I am sending you the file now. We believe that troops are being massed for a military action against the Government. You will get your heavy armor moving also, just as soon as you get confirmation of troop movements in that area. Report back to me within the hour."

Colonel Davis immediately dispatched a surveillance drone to the coordinates provided by General Abrams. He joined the field commander in the IT section to watch the images. They were disturbing. The drone transmitted back images of the base: there was a lot of activity, trucks loaded with troops were travelling in convoy into the base, the uniforms were black; inside the perimeter masses of soldiers stood in formation, and they were being joined by the fresh arrivals. Squads of soldiers dressed in Army khaki were distributing weapons and body armor to the lines of troops; Davis did a rough count, there was almost a battalion in place and more were arriving every minute. He called General Abram.

"General, you were right. Troops are being assembled within the perimeter of the base and aerial assault aircraft are also being prepared. Someone is getting ready to go to war, sir!"

"Colonel, those troops are Robotoids. They will not stop coming at you even if you call upon them to surrender, even if they are outnumbered a hundred to one. Do you have any suggestions, Colonel?"

"Well if bullets or bombs won't stop them, there is only one way. I have some stocks of non-lethal gas. If we preempt the attack, we might surprise them and they won't have time to put on gas masks. Shall I proceed, General?"

General Abrams looked at Admiral Mendez, he nodded. "Yes, do it now and make sure of it. Have your troops follow up and place all combatants in restraints. The poor devils are not to be blamed for what they were about to do. Keep a bird in the air so that we can see the imagery."

Fifteen minutes later, the images started coming through. Colonel Davis had indeed acted quickly to stop the Robotoid shock troops battalion. The reconnaissance drone showed the canisters falling amidst the ranks of Robotoids; they never budged from their positions. As the gas began to spread on the afternoon breeze, they began to fall. Soon the whole body of men lay unconscious in the Californian sunlight. More canisters were dropped around the other buildings and then Davis's troops arrived by helicopter, wearing gas masks and carrying automatic weapons in case of resistance. They went methodically first through the Robotoids' ranks tying their wrists with plastic handcuffs. Trucks were on their way to take them away, but for now they weren't going anywhere.

David and Nick turned off Interstate 93 onto Highway 318. They followed the highway a ways until they came to a place where it took a sharp right turn, and as the satellite imagery had promised, there was a dusty dirt road that branched off on the left. According to David's old topographic map, this was Nevada 375.

"'Not much of a road, for a State Highway," Nick commented. A faded, hand-painted sign propped up on a pile of rocks pointed down the dirt road, it said simply, 'Rachel', there was no distance mentioned. State Highway 375 ran North West along the edge of the restricted area, but nothing could be seen inside the fences that bordered the road, and probably the military facilities were far beyond the range of an observer at ground level.

What struck them as odd was that the military had embedded vehicle detection loops along the center of the dirt road. Usually these types of detectors were placed at intersections to control the phasing of signals. "Those can only be meant to warn the military of intruders." Nick said.
    "Yes, we will have to make our visit brief if they know we are here. Expect to see hovers at any time now." Sure enough, a few minutes later, a hover overflew them. Obviously, the vehicle ID would be checked out by a satellite link. In this case, the hover had air to ground missiles slung under its wings, in its missile pods, in case hostile action was required, supposedly. "Nick, these boys are serious." The hover circled them repeatedly and then buzzed them before flying away in the direction of Groom Lake.

"That was just to remind us who's in charge out here.''

The town of Rachel was nothing but a small series of abandoned subdivisions that hung from a dirt road that leads towards the Air Base. To call it a highway was far too grandiose, but a sign proudly named it as Extraterrestrial Highway. Probably that was a concession to the tourists. From the south side of the town, another dirt road led off in a south westerly direction, the map said that it was called Back Gate Road. They decided that they would pass up the chance to explore that road. The gate was sure to be manned and there was little to be gained by exciting the interest of the authorities in broad daylight.

It seemed that nothing had changed in these parts for the last hundred years, at least anything in a positive way. There were no obvious signs that the presence of a huge military complex just nearby had benefitted the town one iota. David's gazetteer said that Rachel had a population of three hundred at the last census, but there weren't any of them about as they entered the town. The town was dying. Now it consisted of only half a dozen trailers on the roadside, and a gas station that had a single pump which was powered by solar electricity. There was also the Little A' Le'Inn bar and motel, that too had an array of solar panels across the whole of its roof.

They stopped and got gas, and then they went over to the Little A' Le'Inn to wash the desert dusts down. There were no other customers in the bar and the only occupant lay asleep with his head on his folded arms on the counter top. They tapped gently to wake him up and he slowly came around. He greeted them blearily,

"Howdy guys, can I get you something?" They ordered a beer each and he stuck the bottles without glasses in front of them. The price was triple what they might have paid in Las Vegas, but they smiled with good humor as they handed over the notes; the little old man behind the counter just laughed when David told him that they had just got buzzed by a hover. He said, "Most likely they were just doing training maneuvers. They often do that when they see a car on the road. It's just a bit of fun and it lets you know that big brother is watching over you. Nobody ever gets hurt, not yet anyways."

He was a proper character and he'd lived out there all his life. His name was Alf. Probably Alf didn't get out much, he definitely needed to visit a dentist, as he had lost most of his teeth, and his dungarees were patched all over. He got by selling the Alien souvenirs, and gas to the tourists. Not many folks stopped the night; David and Nick guessed that it was because of the security patrols by the hovers and being buzzed by the occasional fighter jet.

Alf warned them that it wasn't a good idea to venture much beyond Rachel, as the cops were likely to do more than just warn you off. David assured them that they were just passing through, just curious, you know, because of the stories in the past about aliens and abductions in this area. He told Alf that his place was famous now, it was recommended as a stopover by several Alien web sites. That pleased Alf no end.

"So Alf, have you ever seen an alien yourself? Some of these UFO nuts reckon that this area is a real hotspot. That's what they say, isn't it Nick?" Nick nodded sagely.

"Nah, look that's just foolish talk! I don't believe in them, even if I make my living selling those daft posters and other alien souvenirs. Hey, don't tell anyone that I told you this," he paused and peeped behind him through the window, to check if there was anyone outside listening, "but only last week, a group of about fifty men marched down the road from the base, mind you that's 24 miles as the crow flies, not an easy thing to walk with packs in this heat! Anyway, they didn't seem to be bothered by it and the packs on their backs were huge. I was curious when I heard the sound of marching feet and I went outside to take a better look. They looked sort of odd. They didn't seem to focus their eyes when they looked at you, you know like the druggies down in Las Vegas!"

"What do you reckon, Alf, were they on drugs? Did they chant one of those marching beats, like the Army do?"

"No, they didn't. That's strange too. The regular army trainees do that to help them combat the fatigue. But these guys just walked in absolute silence, carrying those great big packs. It was real weird, you know? And their uniforms, I've never seen any of our boys dressed in jet black uniforms with berets. No, if they'd had slant eyes, I'd have said they were aliens for sure, real creepy they were! And another thing…they were being shadowed by this huge black painted aircraft. It was triangular in shape, but it made no noise, no noise at all. Now what's that all about?"

Just at that moment the bar door opened and two Army Military Policemen in desert camouflage entered. Alf moved off to the end of the bar counter to serve them. They spoke quietly to Alf, and looked pointedly in the direction of David and Nick. Then they bought a couple of soft drinks and left. Alf waited for a moment until the sound of their Desert Patrollers could be heard and then he sheepishly returned to where David and Nick sat. "You'd best be going, guys. I've been warned off. They don't like strangers around these parts. Sorry, you seem decent enough to me, but I don't want any trouble. Know what I mean?" David and Nick drank up and left within the minute. Down the road, the two Army cops sat on their bikes watching. Then they turned around and returned the way that they had come.

"Look at that, they waited to see whether Alf would send us on our way. Lucky for him that he was smart enough to comply. Nick, it's starting to look very interesting out here, but they have the surveillance tight. This won't be like the San Fernando surveillance. So what do we make of the story about the marching zombies? Robotoids, do you reckon?" Nick nodded.

"Yeh, but you know, David, I'm also interested in the description about the strange triangular plane, it reminded me of something that I had forgotten about. Some years ago, when I was in the Signals, we were assigned to try to detect a top secret new plane. It was designed to be radar invisible but also silent. We had set up lines of sonic detectors all across the desert. These detectors were so good you could have heard a gopher fart; in fact I think we did! Anyway, one of my team actually saw this plane as it flew at low altitude across our network. The detectors didn't hear it, we got no radar image and neither was there a heat trail. Later, someone told me that a plane that had this triangular shape had been developed, it had a zero-gravity propulsion system, which might account for its silent operation. As far as I know, the plane never made it into production, but maybe our General Fraser has got it perfected by now. He was working with General

Browning in the development of new weapons and systems. To me the logical place for that would be out here, in Area 51."

"Well, the presence of Robotoids and high tech weapons is a bad mixture, and one might ask, why are we seeing them now? When the whole Union is preparing to release the detainees and they are saying that they will find a way to restore the Robotoids, why are the military drilling and training Robotoids out here, and under the harshest climatic conditions imaginable?"

"David, we have stumbled onto the General's dirty little secret, he's building an army, that's what. Let's get the hell out of here! You call Duane on a secure line, and tell him what we have found. He will have to act fast, because Fraser knows that time is against him."

Duane answered his call on the second attempt. "Sorry, David, I had company. What have you found out?"

"It seems that Generals Fraser and Browning are training an army of Robotoids. We've seen what they can do before, and they are formidable. When you see troops marching for miles with heavy packs on their backs, you just know that they are for serious business. There was also a reliable report about a huge triangular shaped aircraft that shadowed a group of marching Robotoids. The thing is, the observer said that it was absolutely noiseless, and Nick recalls such a prototype that used a zero-gravity propulsion system. Fraser is surely up to no good, Duane!"

"Then we will have to do something about him. It's a pity that at this stage in the game that we may be looking at a military option, but let just say that it can't be ruled out. There are some big changes coming soon, but Fraser's apparent grab for power is opportunistic. I doubt that the other Joint Chiefs of Staff can be aware of what he is up to. Do we know if he is working alone, David?"

"Nick believes that Browning may be in this with him. He's the scientist, Fraser is more of a technologist and a street fighter, I'm told. Well, if it's a fight he wants, I'm sure that he will get one!"

"Thanks, David and thanks to Nick also. Now get away from there as fast as you legally can. James' man will be standing by to take you to Vegas."

Duane had hardly closed the connection when James came on the line. "Hey, Boss! You will never guess what has happened. You recall the strange story about Herbert Kell? Well, here is the sequel. We were alerted by the local police on Long Island that they had made a routine call at Montague Morgan's place in The Hamptons. It seems that guests to his big bash this morning had blocked the road leading to the Morgan Residence with their vehicles, arrogant sods that they are! Knowing that Morgan can be difficult, a police sergeant accompanied by a beat cop went to request the owners to move their vehicles. There was no one on the gate, which was unusual, but inside the garden they found the guards all dead. Apparently they had all died from massive brain hemorrhages. So they called for backup. A half hour later, at maybe two o'clock in the afternoon, the local police chief and a posse of cops arrived. They feared the worst, but what they saw inside the mansion shocked everybody to the core. No, it was not a bloodbath. But they discovered two hundred or so guests, and Montague Morgan, just standing like rocks. Boss, they are totally paralyzed, every one of them. The only things that move are their eyes. It's so creepy, they are living corpses! The cops took samples of the punch that everyone seemed to have been drinking. The initial results indicate that everyone had been drugged; Morgan even had a needle mark in his upper forehead. Someone injected drugs into his frontal lobe. Now, what do you make of this Duane?"

"Have the Forensics team analyzed the drugs found in the punch bowl or glasses? Did they identify them?"

"Yes, a preliminary finding is that the cocktail of drugs include one that seems to be similar to curare, but not exactly so. However, the other drugs are completely unknown to science."

"James, I know that Jim Stewart had to be behind this: mass brain hemorrhages-that suggests the use of extreme mental pressure, such as a powerful telepath might be able to inflict, and I know that James is a telepath. The unknown drugs have to be from the future, that is why they are completely unknown to science, they haven't been invented yet! Do we have a copy of the guest list, James?"

"Yes we do, Montague had meticulously recorded the organization that each person was affiliated to, their spiritual association and rank. What we have here is the cream of East Coast Society and the Occult world and plenty from the rest of the Union too. Why even the New York Police Commissioner was on the list. It says that he was a leader in a satanic cult! Can you believe that? Jim has taken out the entire power structure of the Illuminati and the other occult groups. In one fell swoop, he has reduced our problems enormously. So what is new from your side?"

"We have discovered trouble with a capital 'T'. David and Nick have confirmed what your operative suspected: General Fraser and General Browning are training Robotoid soldiers and they have other high-tech weapons that I'll bet the rest of the Joint Chiefs know nothing about. If we are right, then Fraser and Browning are going to make a grab for power in the next few days, because it's my guess that they will want to continue to harvest detainees for their military forces!"

In Research Laboratory One, General Browning was giving General Fraser a tour of the facility. Much had changed in the last twelve months and several of their projects had come through field testing and were ready for deployment. Browning had no personal wish for power, his only interests were in the science, technology and developing of new ideas. The arrangement worked well, since Fraser leaned more to action than theoretical ideas and concepts.

"Over here is our accelerated learning module. When you last saw it, it was the size of a large suitcase and we were having problems with the machine-brain interface. We stole some technology from the Chinese actually, and solved the problem. We have reduced the module to this hand held device. We merely place the projecting lens over the eye of the recipient and transmit via a wireless interface which is contained within the headset. The wireless interface between the mainframe and the recipient's brain is very efficient and we have saved on transmission times by having the headset incorporate an unpacking protocol. The upload from the computer now only takes five minutes and the unpacked memories and skill sets which are to be transferred take two hours. I can create a fighter pilot for you in two hours and five minutes, but a less skilled operative, say an infantryman would take only thirty minutes. The limit is that of the number of simultaneous uploads that the computer can handle. We are refining the programming and hopefully, in the not too distant future, we will be able to create

Robotoid warriors in ten minutes, whatever skill set they require."

"And what if we wish to retrain a Robotoid?"

"Oh, that's easy!'' General Browning giggled like a teenager, "We just wipe the implanted memories and reprogram the brain. It's easy peasy.''

"Hmm, then you have created a versatile warrior. So this technology could be applied to normal brains too?''

"Oh, yes. We can reeducate someone to the level that we require. It's only necessary to wipe something that may be alien to the host, say if he or she was required to perform acts that a normal person would find repugnant. I am thinking about acts like attacking civilian populations, or acting as a sexual surrogate. We would prefer to erase those memories permanently. Once we understood how memories were stored electrically, we discovered that it was possible to learn the physical storage address of a certain memory. So it's a bit like reformatting a computer's hard drive, only it's three dimensional storage and the access protocol is a bit complicated.''

A call came in on General Fraser's comm. link, it was the Area Commandant from Los Angeles. Browning paused while Fraser took the call. The news was grave obviously, Fraser's face had hardened into a determined bulldog look. He only made a single comment, "Are you certain, what all of them? Damn!'' He turned to Browning. "Abram and Mendez have wised up to our plan, I can't think how. They have taken out the entire battalion of Robotoids in the San Fernando facility, they dropped gas on them, and it knocked them all out. For now we're finished there. We need your high tech Robotoids now for sure. Carry on with your briefing.''

Browning made no comment but continued as if the interruption had not occurred. "OK, would you like to see a Robotoid operate the flight simulator? We have one over here. Now note how smoothly he transitions in high gravity maneuvers. A normal person would be puking under those vectors, but we have conditioned him to cope. Three hours ago, this Robotoid was doing carpentry on the base, and not very well. He now has the skill and dexterity of a fully qualified fighter pilot. His reflexes are enhanced and he would outperform most pilots in a combat situation."

"What about our new technology weapons? Are the Robotoids trained to use them?"

"Yes, why not? The new weapons are really simpler to use than the conventional ones. The guns don't jam; they are lighter and more ergonomically shaped. See here, this is the new assault weapon. It will fire two hundred rounds of laser pulses, before recharging. It has a range of three hundred yards, and it is equivalent to a machine gun for its rate of fire. The heaviest part of the weapon is the battery pack. We discarded old type batteries as being too heavy and too inefficient. Today's warrior will carry weapons that are powered by lightweight fuel cells. Note that the weapon also has a retractable night scope which has a light intensifier. This weapon is lighter than the regular issue carbine and it is silent, that's its big plus in my view. At night, the warrior will locate his target using the night scope and then only a brief pulse of light will reveal his position. Unless a defender sees the pulse, he will not be able to trace the origin of the shot, since there will be no sound to guide him."

"And we are producing these new weapons here, right? And did you follow through with the heavy caliber laser artillery?"

"Well we don't have a production assembly line yet, but I am working the Robotoids until they drop. By hand assembly, we have ten thousand laser rifles completed so far. Give me another week and I could double that number. But I guess we don't have that long, do we?" Fraser shook his head.

"Oh, well then, we will have to fight smarter. Now here is our pride and joy: the Vulcan Multi-role Combat Fighter, or VMCF. The Vulcan is now battle-ready. It can out fly and outgun anything, anywhere on the planet. It uses the new antigravity propulsion system, so theoretically you could use it for high altitude flight, even near space flights. It has a top speed of Mach 6 and is silent, and sneaky. No radar will find it and its heat signature is negligible. The electronic signatures are cloaked also. We have invented a complete body cloaking system, which is very efficient and does not consume very much power if it is used for short periods. In addition to the conventional weapons, it also carries laser cannons that have a range of twenty miles. It is lethal at half that range. So far we have only one Vulcan that is airworthy. If I had more Robotoids available, I might be able to get two more completed within the month. But I have been concentrating on deploying our resources for ground assault forces, as you indicated that this was our most crucial need. The Vulcan is fueled and ready for flight; we shall be taxiing it out soon, but not in daylight as the Joint Chiefs may be monitoring us by satellite imaging."

"And the pilot, will he be a human or a Robotoid for the maiden operational flight?"

"No a human pilot this time, not that my Robotoids couldn't duplicate his piloting, but we are using this to build the database on flight maneuvers. That is the pilot over there by the open hangar doors, he is wearing the orange flight suit."

"I see, but then, who is that sitting in the cockpit? He's wearing a white suit and he's waving.''

A look of horror swept over Browning's face. He pressed the public address system button and screamed, "Close the doors, close the hangar doors. Security we have an intruder inside the VMCF. Arrest that man!''

The boarding steps of the VMCF retracted and the hatch sealed with a hiss. The security force surged in front of the plane and they used their laser weapons, directing the pulses to the cockpit portal. It was too late, because the intruder had already initiated the lowering of the canopy that would protect the cockpit portal from the laser fire. The Vulcan operates with cameras which are sited around the plane. The powerful engines were fired and the Vulcan moved into its preflight hover position. The intruder swung the plane around until it was facing the closing hangar doors. The klaxon alert warned that the doors would be closed within thirty seconds, and counted it down at ten second intervals.

"Ha, now "we've got you!" General Fraser shouted with his fist in the air. He addressed the pilot over the public address system and via the control channel into the cockpit. "You had better surrender now. The hangar doors are now closed, you cannot escape.''

The only reply that he received, was a laconic, "Hangar doors are now opening." And this was followed by four enormous explosions as the Vulcan's laser cannons opened up on the hangar doors. The power of the four blasts tore the huge doors to shreds, and shards of high tensile metal flew outside. The hangar doors were no more. "Doors are now open." Said the pilot and the Vulcan moved forward, scattering the Robotoids and the other security police before it.

Browning and Fraser looked at each other incredulously.

"Somebody just stole my jet!" Fraser barked, "How could this happen? Get me the Head of Base Security immediately." An aide rushed for the comm. link and demanded that Major Hammond should report to the Research Laboratory Building One immediately.

Major Hammond walked into the control room and, without addressing the two generals; he proceeded to punch some keys on the computer console. The screen showed images of the area previously occupied by the Vulcan. "General Browning, General Fraser this is security footage of the Vulcan over the past twenty four hours. The cameras have continuous multi-spectral images in the hangar. We do not take security lightly. Every technician who entered the Vulcan during this period had to punch in a security code authorization and give a retina scan. The logs show that all entries into the jet were authorized and minor maintenance was carried out during the last twenty four hours. There are no unauthorized entries, into the secure area around the plane or into the plane itself. Here, just five minutes before you detected the intruder we obtained a thermal image inside the cockpit, but the image is somewhat diffused. We don't understand that either. The voice print seems to match that of a security consultant who did a lot of work for us earlier. His name is James Stewart and he is the Managing Director of Stewart Scanners. But he is not in the country; he is in London at this moment. We don't understand how someone could have the same voice print unless he was using a taped message. We are trying to reach Mr. Stewart at this moment on a secure video channel, but so far no luck. But I spoke to his home, and his brother was emphatic that Jim is in England and has no plans for travel to the Union in the near future. I said that I would like to call him and he kindly provided me with a secure number. The man who answered was confirmed by the system security to be Jim Stewart and the system confirmed that he was speaking from London Central."

"Browning, do we know where the Vulcan is now?"

General Browning sniggered, "No, we made a pretty good job of making it untraceable, and we have absolutely no idea of where he is, or how to find him. The pilot seemed to understand the flight controls incredibly quickly. So I am very sure that the plane is in stealth mode and he could be anywhere, even over our heads right now."

As he spoke Jim Stewart's voice came over the control channel. "In a few minutes, I am going to start dropping bombs. I seriously suggest that you evacuate that building immediately." Fraser believed him. Immediately the order to evacuate was sounded throughout the complex and technicians and Robotoids ran for their lives.

Jim gave them the benefit of ten minutes to clear everyone out and then he dropped two of his little bombs on to the laboratory. It was totally destroyed. He then proceeded to do the same to each of the main hangars and buildings within the complex and he used his laser cannons to reduce the remaining facilities buildings to ruins. There were twenty five large buildings when he began, but the explosions from the bombs were so powerful that only craters remained to show that anything had once stood there. General Browning and General Fraser stood looking with dismay upon the work of their own weapon.

"We did this. That madman pulled the trigger, but we did this Fraser." Browning for once showed some backbone in the presence of General Fraser. "You and your crazy ambition! Just look where it has got us! We are ruined." He took a clumsy swing at Fraser, who easily avoided it.

He replied, "You little back-stabber. Don't think that you are going to be able to blame me for all of this. You built the damn weapons; it was you, not me! You have to take your share of the blame and if it is to be a court martial, well there are worse things in life. You could be like one of them for instance."" He indicated a Robotoid who was standing staring vacantly at the sky. Pretty soon, others joined him until more than a hundred had gathered. "What the hell are they looking at?" He grabbed the nearest Robotoid, "You, what do you see?" He could see nothing, only a vague shimmering above the asphalt.

"Plane, Boss." The Robotoid replied, "over there, that's the plane."

Browning became excited again. "Don't you see? They seem to be able to see in the near visible spectrum. That's fascinating. The human brain is indeed a marvelous thing!"

"And we spent ten billion dollars or more to discover that fascinating fact?" Fraser commented sarcastically. The Vulcan approached them. Then Jim switched off the cloaking device and lifted the canopy. He looked out at them. In their minds they heard his voice so clearly.

"You better run. So run!" They ran as hard as they could and as far as they could. They ran until they could run no further. After a quarter of a mile, they collapsed gasping in the shade of some sagebrush shrubs where some Indian Rice Grass offered a soft resting place. But they had hardly caught their breath when Jim's voice chided them again, "Keep going, and don't come back. I'll be waiting here if you do, and I won't be merciful next time. You go and surrender yourselves to the Nevada State Police. Tell them that you've surrendered to the law to face charges of crimes against humanity. If you try to evade this, I will know, and I will find you!"

Duane had by now become used to the sudden appearances of Jim Stewart, which was helped by the certainty that he had brought good news. "Jim, how nice of you to drop in. You have been very busy in the New York area or so I have deduced. Was that your work out at The Hamptons?"

"Well I did pop into a cocktail party, but I left after a short while, they were much too stiff for my liking."

Duane burst into gales of laughter. "Yes, that is certainly true. Will they unfreeze, or shall we put them in the waxworks museum?"

"Now that is an excellent idea, but the intravenous tubes might spoil the dramatic effect, don't you think? I sent Herbert Kell off with a new outlook too. His white hair was quite the look for him. So, I thought about Montie also. You know it would be a terrible shame if you couldn't start off with a clean slate. Those Illuminati and New World Order conspirators would soon be in business before you could even say Kyoto Protocol. So I decided to level the playing field. Don't be surprised if that frozen mob is around for an awful long time. They had a special dose from me of a longevity drug. They will have a long, long time to reflect on the error of their ways. I mean, what is the alternative? You sentence them to a statutory sentence, and they manage to get their time served in a country club, then they are released and it will be business as usual. This way is better, better even than cryogenic incarceration; oh, that will be tried in the future also, but the habitual criminal will always revert to his old ways. Even if they are telepathic, if they have no fear of disclosure, then incarceration is the only recourse. The final solution that mankind will try will be surgical intervention through mind probes. Your General Browning is right on the edge of that technology, by the way, so you'd better watch him."

"Now since you brought his name up, we have a problem. It's both Browning and Fraser, actually. They have been building an army of Robotoids, we think, and developing new technologies. If my advisors are right, then we face a powerful enemy again."

Jim removed his golf ball sized device from his robe and pointed it at the holo-screen, "Not necessarily, my friend. Look at this." The screen showed satellite imagery of a large expanse of desert, at the center of the image, a large number of buildings had been destroyed. Some stood in ruins, still smoking, and craters marked where others had stood. "The Army has just shut down Fraser's facility in the San Fernando Valley; he was massing Robotoid troops there to stage a coup. I dropped General Abrams a note with a crystal showing him what the two conspirators were doing all over the Union. I think that it impressed them. What you are looking at used to be the Groom Lake facility which housed Browning's secret research facility. Today, I destroyed that site with some of my little bombs. I borrowed the Vulcan jet fighter from them to do the job. Listen to the description of this fighter, I recorded their conversation just before I pinched the jet, this is Browning speaking:

'Now here is our pride and joy: the Vulcan Multi-role Combat Fighter, or VMCF. The Vulcan is now battle-ready. It can out fly and outgun anything, anywhere on the planet. It uses the new antigravity

propulsion system, so theoretically you could use it for high altitude flight, even near-space flights. It has a top speed of Mach 6 and is silent, and sneaky. No radar will find it and its heat signature is negligible. The electronic signatures are cloaked also. We have invented a complete body cloaking system, which is very efficient and does not consume very much power if it is used for short periods. In addition to the conventional weapons, it also carries laser cannons that have a range of twenty miles. It is lethal at half that range. So far we have only one Vulcan that is airworthy. If I had more Robotoids available, I might be able to get two more completed within the month.'

Now I used this beast to destroy their installation, and then I stashed it. You are not yet ready for such a weapon; can you imagine what the East Asian Republic would do with it? So I parked it on the moon. Sometime in the future, Jim Stewart will shift his industrial conglomerate to the moon, and he will find the Vulcan, with a short personal note that I have left for him. We don't want them thinking that it was left by aliens do we?" Jim chuckled.

"Did they create any other technology that I ought to know about? Although, unless I can capture Browning, I think that I'm unlikely to find anything useful in the ruins of Groom Lake. "

"Yes, he discovered some ways to insert knowledge directly into the brain. Call it accelerated learning, if you will. Listen to this explanation from Browning:

"Over here is our accelerated learning module. When you last saw it, it was the size of a large suitcase and we were having problems with the machine-brain interface. We stole some technology from the Chinese actually, and solved the problem. We have reduced the module to this hand-held device. We merely place the projecting lens over the eye of the recipient and

transmit via a wireless which is contained within the headset. The wireless interface between the mainframe and the recipient's brain is very efficient and we have saved on transmission times by having the headset incorporate an unpacking protocol. The upload from the computer now only takes five minutes and the unpacked memories and skill sets which are to be transferred take two hours. I can create a fighter pilot for you in two hours and five minutes, but a less skilled operative, say an infantryman, would take only thirty minutes. The limit is that of the number of simultaneous uploads that the computer can handle. We are refining the programming and hopefully in the not too distant future we will be able to simultaneously create many Robotoid warriors in ten minutes, with whatever skill set they require."

"And what if we wish to retrain a Robotoid?"

"Oh, that's easy!" General Browning giggled like a teenager, "We just wipe the implanted memories and reprogram the brain. Easy peesy."

Jim stopped the replay and turned to face Duane, with a serious note in his voice. Now this technology needs to be licensed, it would be so open to abuse, but the potential for benefitting mankind is immense also. Think how you might give remedial schooling to backward kids or impart useful skills to people so that they could be productive in a new vocation. There are many possibilities for good."

"So where are the two rebels now?"

"Where, oh, I think they must be on their way to the Nevada State Police. At least that is where I ordered them to go. They need to give themselves up. Maybe Browning can be rehabilitated, but I'm not so sure about Fraser. In his heart, he wants the power that he tasted in the New White House, but that seat has got your name on it Duane! Now, let's see if we can find them."

The satellite generated image swung east of the Groom Lake facility until it cut Highway 375. Jim increased the magnification until eventually two dusty, stumbling men in uniform could be seen. They had almost reached the highway. "I'll have the cops go pick them up." He fiddled with his device and then turned to Duane with a broad smile on his face. "I've instructed the State Troopers to go arrest these two, and to contact you for instructions. It ought to take about an hour, I guess."

"Jim, on a personal note, may I ask. Since you were transformed to what you are today, and you flit around through space and time, what about your family, and your wife? I expect that you must miss them terribly."

"Duane, thank you for asking. Today, in the future era, Sakura, my wife lives with my sons and several generations of Stewarts. In my early years as a security consultant to the British cabinet, I traveled a lot. Then I met Sakura. We fell in love and I vowed that I was finished with traveling. With the help of my brothers and sons, I built a mighty commercial empire, but I still managed to spend a lot of time with Sakura. Then a situation arose which demanded that I make a sacrifice. Earth was faced with an alien threat that we could not defeat by any normal means. There are some higher beings; you might call them archangels, who offered me a chance to defeat this enemy, but at a price. What you see is the price I paid. I often visit my family but it is too painful for them and me, if I stick around too long. So I decided that my calling was to watch over Earth, and protect my people. I have traveled the galaxy, met with alien species that have impressive civilizations, but honestly, there is no place like home!

Mankind is unique and has many special qualities. You are worth my time. Well, this time I will not just vanish, because this is goodbye, Duane. You do make a good President by the way, but later mankind has to pass through more trials before it reaches what every man is searching for. Farewell, Duane, and I want to thank you for believing in me."

Epilogue

It was now time for the much anticipated introduction of the synthetic version of KP. The protein had been found to enhance brain development and expand intelligence. In laboratory rats the researches had discovered that the offspring of the parents which had received KP enhancements had inherent memory of the testing labyrinths that their parents had passed. Even more amazing, was the discovery that in humans an expansion of intelligence was noted after only drinking a KP solution for one week. But when KP was injected into young children it was more pronounced and the children showed sign of telepathic abilities. The researchers then developed the Kyoto Protocol which was introduced into fertilized embryos. The growing children displayed pronounced telepathic abilities and greater intelligence from a young age. Jim Stewart and his half-Japanese wife, Sakura, were the biological parents of three remarkable children, Grace, Akemi and Akiyoshi. The two girls and a boy were the chosen instruments to bring down the dictators of Euro Zone, East Asian Republic and various countries in South America and Africa. The World Congress, which was held every four years, was the best chance to topple the assembled dictators but the strategy didn't stop at that. The resistance leaders, who included Duane Richards, planned to bring about permanent social change by the introduction of KP into every household.

About every city, the municipal governments have set aside reserves for the supply of water to the population. These reservoirs are connected to water treatment stations and then by a network of pipes the water is distributed to industrial and domestic users. In the treatment stations, the water passes through various filters: chemical and biological. The pollutants are separated and then, when the water has met the specified purity, it is released into the water supply grid. The engineers can only screen for certain known pollutants and it is necessary to keep the list of pollutants up to date. However, the synthesized KP was a new compound and so it passed undetected into the water supply. The majority of the world's population in 2100 lived in urban areas. The seismic incidents of 2050 had resulted in the replacement of coastal cities by new mega-cities. In rural areas, where piped water was still unavailable, the population relied upon lakes, rivers and wells for their water needs. So in introducing the new KP protein into the urban areas, a small proportion of the population would not have access to water that had been treated by the resistance movements.

Very few adverse effects were noted after the population had drunk the enhanced water. After three days, the iris area began to show an intensification of color. By seven days, telepathic awareness had emerged: KP had actually released a latent ability of the brain, and the younger that the recipient was, the more pronounced the gift became.

This had profound societal effects. Criminals discovered that their thoughts were being broadcasted to every person in the vicinity. This led to a rise in lynching and old scores were settled on the basis of the telepathic confessions of the offenders. Instead of ushering in a new era of peace and stability, the legacy of the old ways had to be addressed.

Duane called a meeting of the representatives of the city councils, the military and the American Eagles as well as the smaller resistance groups who operated in the West. It felt that it was the right time to settle upon a plan for the future. Until now his dual role had remained a closely guarded secret, but that was no longer possible, since he too was broadcasting his thoughts uncontrollably. The meeting was convened at the New Washington Convention center, and ten thousand delegates were expected to attend. Duane assumed the role of Chairman.

"Ladies and Gentlemen, delegates and members of the military leadership and Joint Chiefs of Staff. You are most welcome here today for this important congress. Most of you have experienced disruption in both your personal and public lives as a result of the release of telepathic abilities into our nation. I might add that all over the world, other leaders have to face up to the same issues. Civil strife and insurrection may overtake us if we do not see clearly the way through this transitional period. We did not think about this situation at the beginning of the struggle for freedom. Yes, you heard me correctly. I, Duane Richards, have participated in the fight for freedom. Those close to me will attest that I am not lying. I am the leader of the American Eagles."

The delegates erupted in a clamor, most were genuinely shocked at his disclosure. Duane raised his hand for quiet, so that he might continue. "Thank you. Now in dark times such the last fifty years, we had to fight the dictators and other persons who sought to perpetuate the enslavement of our nation under the pretext of the Emergency Powers Declaration. The Freedom Party was the vehicle that enabled Tyler, Sanchez and Sharpe to remain in power. I also wish to tell you that I have in my possession, a confession signed by President Benjamin Tyler. He wrote it moments before he committed suicide, and he regretted two things principally: that he had sold away his integrity to a group called the Olympians; he also repented for turning his back on the religion of his father. They have all gone now: the Freedom Party, the three dictators and the Olympians.

We, who have gathered here today, have a golden opportunity to make a new beginning. We shall have to make bold decisions, learn to forgive those who have wronged us and sincerely work hand in hand to that goal of rebuilding our nation. The Joint Chiefs of Staff wisely saw that we needed to establish a National Reconciliation Tribunal. They were right, we need to be reconciled. However, the guidelines for the Tribunal need to be agreed upon. Now, with your awakened telepathic abilities, you can be empathic to each other. I don't expect a return to the old party politics, they led us nowhere! We can know for the first time maybe, that everybody is speaking from their heart and agreements ought to be easier to make than before the KP revolution.

Finally, we shall need positive government, a clear vision for the path to prosperity. Therefore, I wish to announce to you today, that I am throwing my hat into the ring. I shall stand for the vacant seat of President of the Union of the Americas. We are taking freedom back!

Someone shouted from the floor, "What you said is correct. But there are thousands of our fellow citizens rotting in the detainee camps. Some of them slaving away, even now in factories which are owned by the elite super wealthy class. There are those who are incapacitated, their minds destroyed by injections that rendered them as dumb beasts. What are you going to do for them, Mr. President?"

"First of all, thank you for your endorsement! Believe me that what I have to tell you is on good authority. The mindless individuals, the so-called Robotoids, will be restored. We have technology that will assist in this, but KP will rebuild the old pathways in the brain. Also, the detainees will be reviewed, their arrest records will be checked and provided that there are no legitimate criminal charges or illegal immigration charges pending, we will authorize mass releases. Those workers who wish to continue in employment will be paid for their labor and it will be a fair wage. No more slavery in the Union!"

The delegates gave him a thunderous standing ovation. Senator McDonald stood to address the congress. "Ladies and gentlemen, I think that we need to address these issues immediately. We must appoint discussion leaders and committees to examine the issues. We shall not leave here until we have agreed guidelines for the Tribunal. We will need to agree on the model of government that will meet our needs. I agree that the old confrontational two party system didn't work very well, and since the Olympians were manipulating the whole system for their own benefit, we need a new start. I also think that I shall second the nomination by our brother over there. Duane Richards for President, all in agreement raise your hand!" The vote was unanimous.

In New York City, a fleet of chiller trucks made the transfer of their cargos to the new special wing of the Bell View Hospital. Two hundred and twenty bodies were taken inside on gurneys and delivered to the new mental wards on the top floor. The staff was delighted to see so many celebrities in their hospital. One by one they posed for photos with the Mayor of New York and the Governor. The ladies draped themselves suggestively across the shoulders of the Chief Justice of New York and other famous personalities. It was the highlight of the day. Then as the footsteps of the Director were heard coming down the corridor, it was back to business. The nurses and orderlies roughly stripped the bodies of their clothes and hooked them up to intravenous feeding tubes. No one seemed to care whether the new patients were male or female; as a temporary provision they were placed side by side, two to a bed; they weren't going anywhere that was for sure, not for a very long time.

Glossary of Terms

Albert Pike

Albert Pike (1809-1891) was born on Dec 29. He was a very accomplished man and multi-talented. He rose to prominence as a lawyer; he was a historian, as well as a general. He attained the rank in the Confederate Army of Brigadier General. He authored several Masonic books, one of which was entitled, *'Morals and Dogma'*, he is also widely believed to be the secret author of *The Protocols of the Learned Elders of Zion*; he also composed the ritual for the concordant body, founded the Freemasonry branch known as The Scottish Rite, Southern Jurisdiction, and in 1859, he was elected Sovereign Grand Commander of The order of The Scottish Rite.

Other appointments and freemasonry honors conferred upon him include: The Grand Orator of the Grand Lodge of Arkansas, and he sat as chairman of numerous committees and boards, including the position of Grand Representative over several Freemasonry Jurisdictions.

The 33rd degree of Masonry was created by Albert Pike. He made no secret of his practice of the Luciferian religion and he is credited with being the founder of the Ku Klux Klan. The K.K.K. is an organization which has historically tortured and killed men solely because of the color of their skin. Considering his demonic roots, this comes as no surprise.

Pike taught the significance of Numerology, which is fundamental to an understanding of secret society codes and occult rituals. The numbers 3, 11, 33 and 66 are highly significant in the

Illuminati. K is the 11th letter, so KKK represents 33.

Antichrist

Albert Pike laid the foundations for The New World Order. His fellow Luciferians of today are preparing the world for a New World Order under the leadership of a man. Speculation about who it may be is futile, but the person with spiritual understanding is encouraged to 'calculate':

Here is wisdom. Let him who has understanding calculate the number of the beast, for the number is that of a man; and his number is six hundred and sixty-six. Revelation 13:18

The following explanation comes from www.escapeallthesethings.com and it's the best that I have seen so far:

The answer to these questions comes from an understanding of the ancient classic languages of Hebrew and Greek. As you may recall, the numbers we use today are Arabic or Roman numerals. Like Hebrew and Greek, English has no numerals of its own. In ancient times, before there were Arabic and Roman numerals, a simple decimal system was used for each letter. That is, the first ten letters were given the value of one through ten in ascending order. The next letter, however, was not an eleven, but instead, twenty. Thereafter, each letter was ten more (20, 30, 40, etc). At one hundred, the letter incremented by 100's, (200, 300, 400, etc). Both Hebrew and Greek contain 22 letters. So, the greatest value of any letter (Tav in Hebrew, Omega in Greek) was 400. The ancients simply used letters in place of numbers to indicate numerical values.

Archaeology has found, for example, where a man etched a secret message in stone by saying, "I love the girl whose name equals 545." It is a very simple system and can easily be adapted to English as well.

When John wrote his prophecy giving the value of 666 to the name of the beast (anti-messiah), the ancients had no difficulty understanding the intent. This would be a confirmation of a particular name and would help in the identification process. The key word calculate also adds to the mystery as it is more technical than the simpler word "count." The word "number" in the Greek is "arithmos." The origins of the word "arithmetic." To sum it up (excuse the pun), this verse of Scripture emphasizes that wisdom and understanding must be employed to draw a proper conclusion. Here is wisdom. Let him who has understanding...

Black Gold

Gold that cannot be traced through certificates of origin. The largest source of such gold is alleged to be that which was stolen by Japanese and German armies during WWII. It is estimated that as much as 90,000 tons of pure gold was liberated from these sources in Asia and Europe and then removed from the caches during Operations Black Eagle and Hammer. The name of Ferdinand Marcos keeps cropping up, and a gentleman called Severino Garcia Santa Romana is documented as holding 8,000 metric tonnes of gold bullion of unknown origin in various Swiss bank vaults. Marcos allegedly got hold of Santa Romana's assets, through misuse of a power of attorney, when Sta. Romana died. But since Mr. Santa Romana is also alleged to have been the Illuminati's representative, this was not a smart thing to do. (see Illuminati below)

Bomblettes

The ordnance is classified as an airdrop weapon, the weight of the ordnance depends on the era; for example in World War II, a bomblette weighed approximately 8.5lbs, but they may be smaller. Bomblettes are point initiated, which means that they detonate on contact with the target. A bomblette may contain small metal fragments such as ball bearings which will fire off in every direction causing damage; alternatively, each bomblette may be a mini-bomb filled with a powerful explosive or nerve gas. This type of ordnance is designed to hurt people, similar to a nail bomb.

The bomblettes in the story are of each type.

Degrees of freedom (mechanics):

Wikipedia defines it as follows: *In mechanics, the degree of freedom (DOF) of a mechanical system is the number of independent parameters that define its configuration. Degree of freedom is a fundamental concept central to the analysis of systems of bodies in mechanical engineering, aeronautical engineering, robotics, and structural engineering. It is the number of parameters that determine the state of a physical system.*

The position of a single car (engine) moving along a track has one degree of freedom, because the position of the car is defined by the distance along the track. A train of rigid cars connected by hinges to an engine still has only one degree of freedom because the positions of the cars behind the engine are constrained by the shape of the track.

An automobile with highly stiff suspension can be considered to be a rigid body traveling on a plane (a flat, two-dimensional space). This body has three independent degrees of freedom consisting of two components of translation and one angle of rotation.

Skidding or drifting is a good example of an automobile's three independent degrees of freedom. The position of a rigid body in space is defined by three components of translation and three components of rotation, which means that it has six degrees of freedom.—Wikipedia

Freemasonry

Freemasonry is a secret order with links at the highest degrees of membership to the Luciferian religion of Mithraism, a Persian idolatrous worship system. The freemasons claim descent from the Free Guild of Masons, an artisans' association, but this is untrue. The Secret order has links with The Knights Templar, The Knights of Malta and others. Members progress in the order by following ritualistic formulas which have been handed down, and upon completion of their vows the initiate receives an apron which carries a significant motif; for example, the 9th degree apron features a picture of a hand holding a knife beside a man's severed head, the message is obvious. The highest degree in the freemasons is the 33rd degree, which is a highly significant number in freemasonry, as are 3, 7, 11, 13 and multiples of 33. The highest position that a freemason could attain to would be that of the Devil's (Lucifer's) representative on Earth. According to the Bible, this man has the number 666. The Bible however says that 6 is the number of a man, so 666 merely reinforce the message that the Anti-Christ is not God, but a mortal man. Examples of occult numerology are found in the masonic usage; e.g. Albert Pike, who was a confessed Luciferian (666,) created the 33rd degree of masonry and founded the KKK (11+11+11).

IED:
An improvised explosive device (IED), also known as a roadside bomb, is a homemade bomb constructed and deployed in ways other than in conventional military action. It may be constructed of conventional military explosives, such as an artillery round, attached to a detonating mechanism.

IEDs are often used in terrorist actions or in unconventional warfare by guerrillas or commando forces in a theater of operations. In the second Iraq War, IEDs were used extensively against US-led Coalition forces and by the end of 2007 they had become responsible for approximately 63% of Coalition deaths in Iraq. They are also widely used in Afghanistan by insurgent groups, and have caused over 66% of the Coalition casualties in the 2001–present Afghanistan War.—Wikipedia

Illuminati:
According to the Conspiracy Archive Website: *The proper name of this group is the Illuminati, Order of the Illumined Wise Men. May 1, 1776, was the most important date in Freemasonry's Luciferic New World Order Plans. On that date, an obscure Jesuit-trained professor of Canon law at the University of Ingolstadt in Bavaria, named Adam Weishaupt, founded a secret society called the Ancient and Illuminated Seers of Bavaria. Illuminati were founded on a mixture of:*

- *Masonic secrets (Luciferic Doctrine)*
- *Islamic Mysticism (Sufism)*
- *Jesuit mental discipline (similar to Hatha Yoga)*

A unique and dangerous element was its scientific use of the drug, hashish, to produce an "illuminated" state of mind-derived directly through the Knights Templar's association with the Order of the Assassins *(circa 1050 AD). Illumination had long been a cherished component of Masonry and other occult groups. The Masonic candidate requests, and is promised "light in Masonry." As he goes up the ladder of initiation, he receives "more light". It is because of this society's emphasis on illumination that the AISB became known by its more common title, **the Illuminati**. The term Illuminati, is the plural of the Latin, Illuminatus, meaning "one who is illuminated." Thus, it means a person who has received the full extent of the initiation that is available through Freemasonry. Technically, an Illuminatus is a Master Mason who has received all the "light" Masonry can bestow. He is beyond 32nd ° and perhaps even beyond 33rd °!*

Such people are known as the Masters of Masters of the Temple, and collectively are known by several names other than the Illuminati.

It is commonly alleged that The Illuminati are connected with European Royalty and nobility, and some ascribe leadership to the British Royal Family because of their well publicized strong links with freemasonry. The author believes that the term 'Olympians' applies to this Order.

Since the beginning of the twentieth century, the ancient nobility was joined by prominent super-rich individuals, who were more susceptible to pressure from above because their power derives from material wealth. In the event of disobedience, such members when threatened with the loss of their money and assets would be forced to toe the line. It is believed that many of the members who came from ancient nobility have been replaced by such super-rich individuals.

It is also a common misconception that The Illuminati are the supreme council of the New World Order, nothing could be further from the truth; there are at least two levels above them, each more steeped in evil and possessing occult powers far greater than those possessed by the member of the Illuminati.

Lucifer:

According to the Bible, Lucifer was a high echelon angel, a created being, 'the cherubim that covereth'. The name means 'Light-bearer'. He aspired to be the ruler of Heaven and rebelled. In his rebellion $1/3^{rd}$ of God's angels allied with him. According to Luciferian doctrine the divine roles are reversed: "*The Masonic religion should be, by all of us initiates of the high degrees, maintained in the purity of the Luciferian doctrine. . . Yes, Lucifer is God, and unfortunately Adonay (Jesus) is also God. For the eternal law is that there is no light without shade, no beauty without ugliness, no white without black, for the absolute can only exist as two Gods: darkness being necessary to light to serve as its foil as the pedestal is necessary to the statue, and the brake to the locomotive. . ."The doctrine of Satanism is a heresy; and the true and pure philosophic religion is the belief in Lucifer, the equal of Adonay (Jesus); but Lucifer, God of Light and God of Good, is struggling for humanity against Adonay, the God of darkness and evil.*" From A.C. De La Rive, *La Femme et L'Enfant dans la Franc-Maconnerie Universelle*, p. 588; Lady Queenborough, *Occult Theocracy* pp. 220-221.

RFID:

A radio frequency identification tag (RFID) listens for a radio frequency and responds by transmitting a unique ID, typically a 64 bit identifier yielding 18,000 trillion possible values. A RFID may be a passive device worn as an external tag or a device that is implanted under the skin so that the bearer will be automatically identified when passing a scanner, e.g.

when checking-out in a supermarket or in place of using a credit card at ATM cash machines. A recent Japanese invention has converted a powder into a RFID device, thus enabling currency coated with the powder to be traced, so hoarding cash will be difficult in the New World Order.

Robotoid:
There are differing definitions of what is a Robotoid. Wikipedia describes the process as follows: *Robotoid technology is being made to make nearly exact copies of important people. 'One organization that allegedly uses such classified technology is the Illuminati. Robotoids are "manufactured" first by copying the memory of an entire brain. A holographic image is made of the host's brain and that is transferred into the biological matter functioning as a brain of the Robotoid, but adjustments have to be taught and programmed into the mind of the Robotoid since the body and brain of the Robotoid are not identical to the original person being copied.'*

On the other hand, Zbigniew Brzezinski, Jimmy Carter's National Security Advisor, in his book, entitled, 'The Technotronic Era', spoke of the creation of Robotoids through chemical imprinting: '*Finally, looking ahead to the end of the century, the possibility of biochemical mind control and genetic tinkering with man, including beings which will function like men and reason like them as well, could give rise to some difficult questions.*'

The latter approach is the focus of current research and is the definition used in this story.

Royal Secret
The Royal Secret of freemasonry, which is revealed only to the initiates of thirtieth degree to thirty third

degrees, is that the religion of freemasonry worships Lucifer as god. Albert Pike (see above), who was a leading freemason and Luciferian, instructed the teachers to substitute 'God' in place of 'Lucifer' in order that the lower degree members would be kept in ignorance of the truth. To read the aims and vows then of the lower orders make them appear innocuous, even commendable.

The Royal Secret is that the 32nd degree freemason, often unknowingly, is baptized and consecrated to the service of Lucifer.

The instructor of the 32nd degree informs the initiate, *'From the 32nd degree ritual we are informed of **Agni** who was borrowed from the Hindu worship of **Lucifer** or **Mitra** before the Persians named him **Mithra**. **Agni**, **Indra**, and **Vishnu**: Fire, Light, and Heat, the first trinity and their manifestation in the skies. The interpretations of these symbols will reveal the Holy Doctrine. The one great idea from which they have been unfolded is the Royal Secret.'*

Few appreciate as they should the basis of its claim to exalted morality making it the law for their daily lives, and fewer care for and value the great truth of its philosophy and religion. *'You are not doing an idle thing to learn the Royal Secret. The Aryan kinsmen of our ancestors.... so worshipping their Deities, and creating Light, what should ascend to the skies to invigorate and replenish Indra, the universal light, the planets and stars that had once been men, their ancestors.'*

The symbols of Free Masonry conceal, even in the Master's Lodge, the Holy Luciferian Doctrine and the Royal Secret.

Satan:

Another name of Lucifer, he also goes by the name of Beelzebub. The name Satan, and its feminine form **Sitnah**: come from the verb which means to resist or be an adversary. Thus the name is descriptive of his actions and character rather than a proper name. Previous to his expulsion from heaven, (Job 1:6, Revelation 12:9), he is thought to have been an anointed cherub or ex-cherub, but descriptions of his anatomy suggest that he may have been a leader of the worship to God since he had built in horns and organs that produced percussion. (Ezekiel 28:14, has been interpreted as relating to Satan, although it apparently refers to the king of Tyre, the context is obviously about a lot more). We know that he led an insurrection, and 1/3rd of God's angels fell with him. Biblical references suggest that his angelic following is hierarchical in the same way that God's Kingdom is organized. Suffice to say that he poses no threat to God and Satan certainly does not merit worship as a deity.

Christ's victory over Satan at His resurrection is a victory obtained for mankind. There is no indication that God and Satan ever came to blows personally. Satan is not omnipresent and not omnipotent or omniscient. He has no ability to create, and indications are myriad that he is not even able to govern or manage well any large number of creatures, except through coercion and fear. Nothing that is commonly ascribed to Satan (darkness, fire, evil) actually belongs to Satan, as everything belongs to God; the entire world (Psalm 24:1), and all souls (Ezekiel 18:4). Sourced in part from http://www.abarim-publications.com/Meaning/satan.html

Spy Bug

Author's note…When I wrote this story, I didn't know about the following facts…life imitating fiction? "It's an insect spy drone for urban areas, already in production, funded by the US Government. It can be remotely controlled and is equipped with a camera and a microphone. It can land on you, and it may have the potential to take a DNA sample or leave RFID tracking nanotechnology on your skin. It can fly through an open window, or it can attach to your clothing until you take it in your home." Source - a news item on Google Plus of Sept 7th 2012.

Lightning Source UK Ltd.
Milton Keynes UK
UKOW04f1140141114

241610UK00004B/98/P